THE GAME

Leslie McGill

SADDLEBACK
EDUCATIONAL PUBLISHING

CAP CENTRAL

Fighter
Running Scared
Hacker
Gearhead
The Game
Hero

www.sdlback.com

Copyright © 2015 by Saddleback Educational Publishing
All rights reserved. No part of this book may be reproduced in any form or by any means, electronic or mechanical, including photocopying, recording, scanning, or by any information storage and retrieval system, without the written permission of the publisher. SADDLEBACK EDUCATIONAL PUBLISHING and any associated logos are trademarks and/or registered trademarks of Saddleback Educational Publishing.

ISBN-13: 978-1-68021-045-3
ISBN-10: 1-68021-045-9
eBook: 978-1-63078-351-8

Printed in Guangzhou, China
NOR/0615/CA21500931

19 18 17 16 15   1 2 3 4 5

To special education teachers everywhere

CECILIA

Cecilia Calhoun opened the door to the girls' locker room. She almost bumped into Remy Stevenson. Remy was standing about three feet from the door. He practically blocked the doorway. The rest of the step team pushed up against Cecilia as they tried to leave.

"Brennay! Your lover is here waiting for you!" Zakia Johnson called out in a singsong voice. Several of the girls laughed. Remy didn't respond. He scanned the crowd of girls leaving the locker room.

Cecilia knew he was looking for Brennay Baxter, captain of the Stepperz, the Capital Central High School step team. Remy idolized Brennay. He waited for her every day. Most days, Brennay just told him to go home.

Brennay pushed through the crowd of girls. "There you are, Remy!" she said sweetly. "I'm so glad! Did you bring me your Washington Wizards sweatshirt like I asked you to?"

Remy handed over a sweatshirt.

"You ready?" Brennay said to Zakia.

Zakia pulled out her cell phone. "Go for it," she said, holding it out to use the camera.

Brennay put on the sweatshirt. Then she reached up and hugged the tall, skinny boy. "My hero!" she said.

Remy looked uncomfortable. He stared at the floor. Zakia snapped a picture.

More points for Lady Bay, Cecilia thought to herself.

Remy was the focus of an online game. Someone had started a blog called *Cap Central Chatter*. The blog reported on all the gossip: who had hooked up, fights, complaints about teachers, and other tidbits going on at school. The last item in the blog each time was the same: a chart labeled "Remy Points."

Under the chart's title was a list of girls' nicknames. Points were awarded for interactions with Remy Stevenson. Last night's installment had given four points to "Z-Grrrl" for taking Remy's e-reader. The day before, "Lady Bay" received three points. Remy had put his arm around her.

The blog even listed "official" rules for how the Remy Points would be awarded. All points had to be documented by a picture sent to the blog's moderator. The photos weren't actually published. The moderator—whoever he or she was—awarded the points and updated the total for each name.

So far, Lady Bay was in the lead with thirty-two points. Cecilia assumed that Lady Bay was Brennay. Z-Grrrl, who had twenty-eight points, had to be Zakia Johnson, Brennay's best friend and co-captain. Cecilia suspected that Brennay and Zakia wrote the blog, invented the game, and were holding on to all the photos.

Cecilia knew the super-sweet tone Brennay used with Remy was a lie. The whole purpose of the game was to get laughs at Remy's expense. Everyone at Cap Central was in on the joke.

Everyone except Remy Stevenson.

Remy truly believed Brennay when she told him she loved him.

Believed her when she called him her hero.

Thought she meant it when she said he was the step team's good luck charm.

Remy believed everything Brennay said. He didn't hear the insincerity or the fawning tone.

Because Remy was autistic.

Cecilia knew people with autism had trouble reading social cues. They had trouble understanding the meaning behind other people's words or expressions.

For the past several years, Cecilia had volunteered at Crossroads, an after-school program for little kids with special needs. Many of the children she worked with were autistic. She enjoyed the work so much that she had already decided to be a special education teacher. She would have done anything to protect the children she worked with from bullies.

Yet here at Cap Central, she was a member of a team whose captain was using an autistic boy as the focus of a cruel game. A boy who didn't understand that the girl he idolized was just pretending to like him.

Every time she saw Remy with Brennay, Cecilia vowed she would put a stop to the game. She knew she should tell a teacher at the school what was happening. But as captain of the Stepperz, Brennay had a lot of prestige. And it seemed like the whole school was in on the game.

Cecilia had moved into the neighborhood near Capital Central over the summer. She still didn't know other students well enough to enlist their support. The girls she knew best were the Stepperz. They went along with anything Brennay suggested. The last thing Cecilia wanted to do was turn in the only girls she'd gotten to know so far.

And she really didn't even know whom she could tell. Mrs. Hess, Capital Central's principal, relied on the Stepperz to entertain at pep rallies, fund-raising kick-offs, and other school events. Her support had to mean she approved of the team, its activities, and its captains.

Cecilia wished she could come up with a way of making Brennay, Zakia, and the rest of the school understand how wrong the game was. Or even just a way to make it stop. She hated herself for being so weak. By not doing anything to stop the game, she felt like she was no better than those who played it.

She felt helpless.

And angry.

And disgusted.

With herself most of all.

CHAPTER 2

MARCUS

Check out Brennay," Eva Morales said, looking across Cap Central's cafeteria to a table crowded with girls. "She's practically sitting on Remy Stevenson's lap."

Marcus DiMonte turned in his seat to look at Brennay. Remy Stevenson sat in the center of a table filled with Cap Central step team members. Brennay sat close to him, stroking his arm. Remy stared at his tray, not responding. His face did not show how he felt about the attention.

"Trying to rack up more Remy Points," Lionel "Ferg" Ferguson said as he sat down beside Marcus. Ferg and Eva had been a couple for several years. Both were a bit large.

Marcus shifted his chair a few inches to give Ferg more room.

"I hate that game," Eva said. "I don't think any of the Poms are playing it. Remy's always with the Stepperz, so I'll bet Lady Bay and Z-Grrrl and the rest are step team members."

The poms team, which did dance routines using pom-poms, was just getting started. The step team had been around for years. It was well-known in the community. The Stepperz were often asked to perform in parades and various events around Washington, D.C. They had even performed in the last presidential inaugural parade.

"Looks like he's in heaven," Ferg said with a laugh. He unwrapped his hamburger and ate it in three bites. He picked up Eva's hamburger off her tray. "You eatin' that?" he asked.

"Give it back!" Eva said, grabbing it. "Yes, I'm gonna eat it. That's why I bought it."

"I'm still hungry," Ferg said, looking down the line at everyone else's tray. "Anybody got—"

"Don't even think about it!" Marcus said, covering his tray with his arms. "Go buy something else."

"Room for two more?" asked Joss White, Eva's best friend, as she neared the table. She was followed by her boyfriend, Carlos Garcia. They put down their trays and sat down. "Did you read in the *Chatter* that Thomas Porter and Brennay are together now?" Joss asked.

"Now there's a combination," Eva said jokingly. "I give that one about a week."

"Yeah, nothing like jail to break a couple up," Carlos added.

Thomas Porter had transferred to Capital Central after a shooting incident at another D.C. high school. Most of the kids considered him dangerous and left him alone.

"Brennay treats Remy like her pet dog. He's showing up more and more in the pictures Brennay posts of the Stepperz. Honestly, I don't know how those girls keep their grades up," Joss said. "Brennay has them stage all sorts of photos, all around D.C. Last week, she had pictures of some of them in the reflecting pool. Remy was in a lot of the pictures."

"Where's the reflecting pool?" Ferg asked. Cap Central was in the Northeast quadrant of Washington, D.C. But the kids who attended the large high school had little contact with the Washington, D.C., that was the nation's capital.

"Downtown, genius," Marcus with sarcasm. "On the Mall. You need to get out more."

"I saw those pictures," Eva said. "I couldn't figure out what they were doing. Or why Remy was all wet. It's not as if you can go in the water down there."

"I saw that too," Carlos said. "I wondered if Remy had fallen in. There were lots of pictures of him dripping wet."

"I know, right?" Joss said. "And after that, the point total increased in that horrible game on *Cap Central Chatter*. Obviously Brennay and Zakia are writing the blog and giving out points. I just can't believe they use Remy that way."

"You'd think they'd have gotten bored by now," Eva said. "Why would they want to keep messing with a kid who's re—"

"I think he's autistic," Marcus said quickly. "He's got special needs. That's all."

"Well, right now he looks like he's got a special need for Brennay," Eva said with a smirk. "Does autistic mean retarded?" she asked.

"Don't!" Marcus said sharply. "Don't use

that word. I know you didn't mean it to be, but it's hurtful."

Eva looked confused. "I'm sorry. I didn't mean anything by it."

"I know," Marcus said. "People don't know. But trust me on that. It's not something you should say. Anyway, autistic means ... well, it means different things to different people."

"I've had Remy in classes," Joss said. "There's something sort of ... well, off about him. I tried talking to him a couple of times, but it didn't go very well. He's just not quite—I don't know. He kept looking to the side of me as I talked to him. I finally gave up." She turned around in her seat and craned her neck to look over the crowd of students eating lunch. "That's why it's so odd to see him hanging out with the step team."

"I thought I saw Remy down at the track last week," Carlos said. "Can someone in special ed be on the track team?"

"Did you actually see him run?" Marcus said with a laugh. "Probably not. He's so fast he's pretty much a blur. Running is a perfect sport for him. Not much social contact or having to read people's intentions by their expressions. Not like in football or baseball. He may one of the top ten racers in the Mid-Atlantic."

"How do you know so much about it?" Joss asked.

"Because I'm a runner too," Marcus said. "And what I usually see of Remy is the back of his jersey as he passes me by!"

"No, I mean the other thing. How do you know so much about autism?" Joss asked.

"Because—" Marcus stopped suddenly, his sentence unfinished. "I just do," he said. He didn't feel like telling his friends about his cousin Sam. Sammy had learning difficulties. He was in special education classes. Many of Sam's classmates were autistic. Marcus loved Sam. He knew how much it hurt when anyone used the word "retarded" to describe him.

Just then, Cecilia Calhoun stood up from where she was sitting. She had been at the very end of the step team's table. She walked over to the trash can.

"Hey, you want this?" Marcus asked, putting a cookie on Ferg's tray. He stood up and picked up his tray.

"Yeah, but what's your hurry?" Ferg asked, grabbing the cookie.

"I'll see you all later," Marcus said. He threw away his trash and walked out of the cafeteria.

He looked down the hallway just in time to see Cecilia disappear behind the wall with the trophy case. He walked around the wall. She was sitting on the floor.

"Hey!" he said, joining her. "You hiding back here?"

"Sort of," she said.

He sat beside her. "Haven't seen much of you lately," he said. "You don't sit on your porch anymore."

Lyman Place was filled with row houses with matching porches. Marcus's family lived at one end. Cecilia's family lived halfway down the block, in a house with a porch swing. Families often gathered on the porches in the summer.

After Cecilia had moved in, Marcus could stand on his porch and look down the row of porches to see her rocking back and forth on her porch swing. He became so used to seeing her there that he automatically looked for her whenever he walked onto his porch.

"Wish it were still summer," Cecilia said, shaking her head. "I had no idea this year would be so hard."

The bell rang, indicating the end of lunch. Cecilia and Marcus stood up. Cecilia brushed off the seat of her jeans.

"Where are you going?" Marcus asked as they climbed the stairs.

"Art," she said. "You?"

"Chem," he said. "Art sounds nice. Wanna switch?"

Cecilia shook her head.

"Hey, it was a joke," he said. "You okay?"

"Yeah. Perfect," she said sarcastically.

"What's up?" he asked with concern.

"Nothing," she answered. "Just a lot on my mind, that's all."

The warning bell rang. Cecilia started for the art room.

"Hey, Cecilia!" Marcus called after her.

She turned around.

"You know I love that porch swing of yours," he said.

Cecilia put her hands on her hips. "You want

it?" she teased with a smile. "I could ask my mom if you could borrow it sometime."

"How about I just use it on your porch?" he responded.

Cecilia tilted her head slightly and looked at him, like she was trying to read something on his face. Whatever she saw seemed to be okay. "Any time," she said with a smile. She gave a little wave and walked into the art room.

Marcus watched her for a moment, then turned the corner to the chemistry lab.

CECILIA

Cecilia stowed her books in her cubby. Then she took her seat at one of the large wooden art tables. Art was her favorite subject, and she was good at it. She had always found it very relaxing to draw. But lately, it seemed like her talent had deserted her.

The class was focused on figure drawing. Her figures hardly even looked like people. Instead of relaxing, she had spent her drawing time thinking about how she could put a stop to the way Remy was being bullied.

"Class, today we are going to concentrate on drawing hands," Ms. Ross said. "Anyone feel like being our model?"

Cecilia raised her hand. At this point, she'd

rather be the model than see once again how badly she was drawing.

"Not you, Cecilia, I'm afraid," Ms. Ross said. "You need to get some practice in. Anyone else?"

"I'll do it," Neecy Bethune said. "Can I just take a nap while they draw my hands?"

"Sure," Ms. Ross said. "Just keep your hands exactly as I place them here, and you can do what you want."

Ms. Ross took Neecy's hands and positioned them the way she wanted.

"Class, let's use charcoal today," the teacher said. "And we're going for realism. I want these hands to be so lifelike you could almost imagine the fingers moving!"

Cecilia got charcoal and drawing paper. She started to sketch. As she drew, her thoughts turned as they usually did to the mess she was in.

The year had started out better than she expected. Cecilia and her mother had moved to the house on Lyman Place after her father had been killed in a car accident. She still missed her father every day, but moving to a new house had helped.

She had worried about changing from the

private school she'd attended all her life to Cap Central. Joining the step team had made the transition easier. She hadn't made any close friends, but most of the step team members were nice to her. The team's activities gave her something to do.

The team was much more active in the community than the step team had been at Cecilia's old school. Brennay Baxter volunteered the team for parades and other events. And she was always coming up with suggestions for photo shoots they could post on Instagram and other social media sites. Although Brennay and Zakia Johnson were co-captains, it was really Brennay who called the shots and controlled the team.

Cecilia really disliked Brennay. She was controlling and demanding. She expected the team members to do whatever she said. She made life miserable for those who challenged her. One girl had disagreed with Brennay at a team meeting. Brennay ordered the others to stay away from her until she apologized. After that, no one dared disagree.

And then Brennay started including Remy in team activities.

At first it seemed innocent. Almost like some sort of service project. Brennay announced at a team meeting that Remy had agreed to be the Stepperz mascot. The girls touched him for luck.

But then the blog started, with the chart of Remy Points. The game put an ugly spin on the team's relationship with Remy. Brennay began being physical with him. Each time she did, Lady Bay rose in the scoring total. Lady Bay and Z-Grrrl had the most points, though some of the other step team members were starting to earn points as well.

Last week before a pep rally, Brennay had insisted that each of the girls kiss Remy for luck. Cecilia did all she could to keep from participating. Brennay noticed and accused her of disrespecting the team mascot. So Cecilia kissed him quickly, trying to ignore the uncomfortable look on his face. Brennay took pictures as each girl kissed him. Cecilia was relieved that so far the pictures hadn't been posted on *Cap Central Chatter*.

Brennay had assured the team that Remy was okay with the attention. Cecilia suspected that Remy would say anything Brennay told him to say. His feelings for Brennay, along with his autism, made him vulnerable to her control.

Cecilia knew the right thing to do would be to tell Brennay to stop. But that wasn't so easy. She didn't want to risk doing anything that would make Brennay angry. It was hard getting to know people at Cap Central. It would be terrible if the few people she knew at this new school were to shun her. She knew she should have spoken more firmly to Brennay when she had told the girls they would all kiss Remy for good luck. She felt like a coward.

But being a coward wasn't the only reason she hadn't pushed it with Brennay. Cecilia had seen the look on Remy's face whenever he looked at Brennay. Clearly, he idolized her. He didn't seem to care what she made him do. Just being with Brennay seemed to make him happy.

Brennay was a bully. She took advantage of someone with special needs. She turned his affection for her into a school joke.

But Remy didn't seem to mind. And that was the problem.

CHAPTER 4

MARCUS

As soon as school let out, Marcus went to the boys' locker room to change. He was early. The only runners there were Remy Stevenson and Durand Butler. Marcus said hello to each, but only Durand responded.

"Hey, Remy, did I see you sitting with Brennay at lunch today?" Marcus asked.

Remy nodded, looking at the floor.

"What's going on with you two?" Durand asked. "I've been seeing you with the step team a lot lately."

"I'm their mascot," Remy said. "They like me."

Durand and Marcus exchanged looks. They both knew Brennay. They knew she was taking advantage of Remy.

"You might want to be careful," Marcus

said. "I think she goes out with Thomas Porter."

"Thomas isn't her boyfriend," Remy said, slamming his locker shut. He left the locker room.

"That's not going to end well," Durand said. "I don't trust Brennay. I'm just surprised the rest of the team is playing her game."

"I know, right?" Marcus said. "I actually thought some of the girls on the team were nicer than that." Cecilia Calhoun flashed into his mind for a moment. "You'd think somebody would put a stop to it."

He and Durand went outside and started warming up. Remy stood alone. He did his warm-ups. The coach gave the boys some instructions, and they all started running. At first the team was in a pack. But they spread out, with the faster runners up front. Remy was in the lead.

Marcus loved to run. He relaxed when he got into a rhythm. He heard someone behind him.

"Hey, did you see those guys standing around talking to Coach?" Durand asked as they ran.

"Yeah, I saw them, but I didn't really pay attention," Marcus said. "Why? Who are they?"

"Somebody said they were scouts," Durand said. "From really good schools too. Stanford,

Michigan, and Georgetown. I think they're looking at Remy."

"They're not looking at us?" Marcus joked.

"Yeah, right!" Durand said, laughing. "That
would be great if they made Remy an offer.
Though I wonder how he would do at college."

"I'll bet they have lots of people who would
help him," Marcus said. "Somebody like that
running for you? They'll do whatever it takes.
He'll probably go to the Olympics some day."

"Maybe if we run real fast, they'll look at
us too," Durand said. "I could use a scholarship
somewhere."

"Problem is, they'll already be gone and
sitting down to dinner by the time we get back
to school." Marcus laughed. "Remy's probably
already back at the locker room, and we're only
half-way done."

At the end of his run, Marcus did his cool-
down stretches. He saw Remy talking to the
three men in suits. Remy was facing Marcus, and
the men were standing around him. Remy looked
uncomfortable, as he often did. Although the men
were talking to him, he wasn't looking at any of
them. Instead, he was looking off to the side.

All of a sudden, Remy looked up with a startled look on his face. Marcus looked around to see what he was looking at. Thomas Porter and Brennay Baxter were crossing the sidewalk. Thomas had his arm around Brennay's shoulders. As he watched, Brennay stood on her tiptoes and kissed Thomas on the lips. She then looked toward Remy and wiggled her fingers in a little wave.

Marcus turned back toward Remy. He looked miserable. He started to walk away but stopped when the coach said something to him. He stood looking at the ground while the men talked.

Marcus saw the three men look at each other. They looked at the coach. Everyone seemed to be a little confused. Coach said something to Remy, who didn't answer. The coach shrugged. He then said something to the men, who nodded and started to leave. One of them held his hand out to shake hands with Remy. Remy never looked up. His hurt feelings were obvious.

Marcus felt bad for Remy. He wished there were a way of protecting him against Brennay's cruelty. He walked into the locker room. As he changed clothes, he thought back to his conversation with Cecilia. He wondered what had her feeling so stressed. He had enjoyed getting to know her over the summer.

He wondered how she felt about the way Brennay was treating Remy. He hoped she wasn't joining in on the teasing. Bullying anyone with special needs was a deal-breaker for him.

Marcus knew having a cousin with learning issues made him more sensitive to bullying. But even if he didn't have Sammy to look out for, picking on someone with special needs was just plain wrong. If anyone took advantage of Sam the way Brennay was taking advantage of Remy, Marcus would do whatever it took to make it stop.

And just standing by while someone else did the bullying was almost as bad. He hoped Cecilia felt the same way.

CHAPTER 5

CECILIA

On Thursday the step team practice lasted later than usual. As soon as Brennay blew the whistle to signal they were done, Cecilia flew to her locker to get her book bag. She had to get to the Trinidad Recreation Center for the Crossroads program.

She loved working with "her" kids. They expected her there, and she didn't like to disappoint them. She hated being late. Mrs. Reynolds, the program director, had recently announced an all-day festival and asked Cecilia to serve on the planning committee. She was pleased to have been given such a responsible role. The extra work, though, added to her already busy schedule.

She had almost reached Cap Central's main

entrance by the trophy case when someone called her name. She turned around. Thomas Porter was standing in the doorway to the boys' restroom. He was holding the door partly open. He looked worried.

"Hey, I need help," Thomas said. "Can you come here?"

Cecilia didn't like Thomas. She tried to avoid him as much as possible. He scared her. He was big and tough looking. Everyone knew he was trouble. Everyone except Brennay.

Brennay told everyone who would listen how much she cared about Thomas. She claimed that he cared equally for her. But she seemed not quite sure she could trust him. She suspected every girl of trying to steal him away.

"Is everything okay? What's the matter?" Cecilia asked reluctantly.

"Do you know any first aid?" Thomas asked. "I think this guy needs help."

Cecilia was certified in first aid. She'd taken a Red Cross training course when she started volunteering at Crossroads. She dropped her bag and ran back to the bathroom.

"In here," Thomas said, holding the door open.

She stepped into the restroom. It seemed to be empty.

"Who needs help?" she asked, looking around. "There's no one else here!"

Thomas pushed her up against the door. He kissed her roughly.

Cecilia was stunned. She tried to push past him, but he blocked her way.

"Seriously, Thomas?" she said sharply. "Get away from me!"

He put his hands on both sides of her head and kissed her again. Some of her braids came loose from the elastic band holding them together. She slid down the door and slipped out of his grasp. She jerked the door open and nearly ran into Brennay.

"Girl?" Brennay said incredulously. "That's the boys' room!"

The door opened wider and Thomas walked out. For a moment, Brennay looked confused. But then her expression changed. Her eyes narrowed and her face grew hard.

"You're going to pay for this," she said to Cecilia.

"But I—" Cecilia started.

"Don't even try," Brennay said. "I know what I saw."

"No!" Cecilia said desperately. "He told me that someone needed help! I never would have—"

"Girl, what are you going on about?" Thomas said, putting his arm around Brennay. "I've been looking for you everywhere."

"Even in the boys' room?" Brennay asked sharply.

"Let's go, baby," Thomas said. He started down the hall, still holding Brennay close. But then he had stopped. He wrapped Brennay in a hug and looked at Cecilia over her head. He winked and grinned.

Cecilia shuddered.

"I've been thinking about you all day long," he said. His eyes were focused on Cecilia. "Fact is, I think about you all the time."

Brennay reached up to kiss him. Then she noticed he was looking at Cecilia. Her expression changed to icy hatred.

"Hang on a second," she said to Thomas.

She walked back down the hall to where Cecilia still stood.

"Brennay, I'm sorry, I—" Cecilia started to say.

"Save it," Brennay said viciously. "You're going to pay for this. Big-time. And when it happens, just remember you brought it on yourself."

"Brennay, please!" Cecilia cried.

Brennay turned and walked back to Thomas. "Let's go, baby," she said sweetly, without a hint of the anger.

Cecilia was shaking as she watched her go. No one had ever spoken to her with such hatred. Brennay scared her. She switched so easily between emotions. Cecilia dreaded the punishment that was coming her way.

CHAPTER 6

MARCUS

Ouch!" Marcus yelled as his young cousin jumped on him. He'd been sleeping soundly.

"Come on, Marcus, let's watch cartoons," Sam said.

Marcus often watched Sam on Saturdays. He loved his cousin and enjoyed spending time with him. Sammy was a sweet little guy who was always cheerful.

"Go turn on the TV," Marcus said. "I'll be there in a minute." So much for sleeping in. He threw on some clothes and went into the living room. "What do you want to do today?" Marcus asked, pouring himself a bowl of cereal.

"I want to practice running," Sammy said.

"Practice running?" Marcus echoed. "Not much to practice. You just run."

"But I need to be fast," Sammy said seriously. "We're having a festival. With races." Sometimes Sammy was hard to understand. Since he started working with a speech therapist, he was easier to talk to.

"Who is?" Marcus asked.

"My after-school class. There's going to be a bouncy castle!"

"I love bouncy castles," Marcus said. "Can I come?"

"Yeah!" Sammy said. But then he looked serious. "But you can't be in any of the races. You're too big."

"Well, that's not fair," Marcus teased. "Who do I have to beat up to be allowed in the bouncy castle?"

Sam looked thoughtful for a minute. "Maybe CeCe," he said.

"Who is CeCe? Is she your girlfriend?" Marcus asked.

"I don't have a girlfriend," Sammy said, punching him. "She's one of my teachers."

"I think she's your girlfriend," Marcus said. "Sammy loves CeCe. Sammy loves CeCe."

Sammy started pummeling him with his fists.

"Hey, knock it off, you two," Marcus's mother said, coming into the room. "Take it outside."

"Come on, Sammy. Let's go practice running," Marcus said.

For the rest of the day, he played with Sam. After dinner, the two cousins sat on the porch and waited for Marcus's aunt to pick up Sammy. In the distance, Marcus saw Cecilia sitting on her porch swing. He stood up to get a better look.

"What are you doing, Marcus?" Sammy asked, looking down the row of porches.

"Nothing," Marcus said. "A friend of mine lives down there, that's all."

"What's her name?" Sammy asked.

"Not telling," Marcus said.

"She's your girlfriend, huh?" Sammy said with delight.

"No, she's not," Marcus said quickly.

"I think she is. You love her! You want to marry her!" Sammy said.

"All right, that's it," Marcus said. He grabbed the little boy and started tickling him. Sammy began shrieking with laughter.

Just then Sammy's mother pulled up. Marcus kissed the little boy goodbye.

"Will you take me to the festival?" Sammy asked as he climbed into the car.

"You bet," Marcus said. "I wouldn't miss it."

Marcus closed the door. As the car drove off, he started down the block toward Cecilia's house.

"Hey," Cecilia said when he got to her steps. "Was that you making all that noise?"

"My little cousin was over today," Marcus said. "He wore me out."

"Want to swing?" Cecilia asked, moving over.

Marcus sat down. He pushed against the floor to make the swing move gently. For a while neither of them said anything. The swing creaked rhythmically. Against the muffled sound of traffic a few blocks away, a few late-season crickets sang.

"There's something sort of sad about this time of year, don't you think?" Marcus asked. "The weather is nice, but there's something different about the light. You just know winter is coming."

"Wish it didn't have to," Cecilia said sadly. "Wish things didn't always have to change."

Marcus heard something in her voice. "What's up?" he asked gently.

"Honestly?" Cecilia said. "I'm just tired of all the—I don't know. Tired of how mean people can be."

"Don't you like Cap Central?" Marcus asked. "You seem to have fit in right away. I'd think being on step team would have given you some instant friends."

"Not friends, actually," Cecilia said. "No one on the team is a friend. In fact, the more I know of them, the less I like them," she added. "Truth be told, so far I haven't made a whole lot of friends. Don't get me wrong, I like you a lot, but besides you, I haven't gotten to know anybody very well."

"So Brennay Baxter's not going to be your BFF?" Marcus asked with a wink. "Actually, I'm glad to hear it."

Cecilia shuddered. "She's may be the meanest person I've ever known," she said. "I hate what she's doing to Remy Stevenson. I think she's the one writing that horrible *Cap Central Chatter*. Brennay and her friends."

"So why hang around them?" Marcus asked.

"I don't," Cecilia said. "I like stepping, so I don't want to quit the team. I just try to stay on her good side. Not go along with her games."

"Games?" Marcus asked. "You mean like Remy Points?"

"Yeah," Cecilia said. "She's getting worse with that stuff. I don't want to have anything to do with it, but he's with the team all the time. She punishes anyone who doesn't go along with her plans for him. She's scary."

"I can't imagine you going along with something cruel," Marcus said. "Can't you just quit?"

"I know I should, but they're really the only people I know," Cecilia said. "I feel like I should do something about the Remy situation. But so far I've been a total wimp about standing up to Brennay. It doesn't make me feel too good about myself. I want to do the right thing. But part of the problem is that Remy doesn't seem to mind."

"Doesn't make it okay, though," Marcus said. "But I know what you mean. I tried talking to Remy. Asked him to stay away from Brennay. He wouldn't listen."

"At least you did something," Cecilia said bitterly. "I've just been trying to stay out of Brennay's way. I feel like a coward."

"Don't be so hard on yourself," Marcus

said. "When the opportunity comes up, you'll do what's right. But let's go back to something you said earlier," he said, lightening his tone. "The 'I like you a lot' part."

Cecilia laughed. "I don't remember saying that," she said.

"I know I heard it," Marcus said. "Sorta made my night, if you want to know." He reached over and picked up one of Cecilia's braids. He used the end of it to tickle her cheek.

"How come you're the only stepper who wears a Cap Central hair thing?" he asked.

Cecilia looked confused. "What Cap Central hair thing?"

Marcus touched the elastic holding back her braids. It had a CC on it. "This," he said.

"But it's not—oh. Wait," she said with a grin. "Those are my initials."

"Well, that's lucky," Marcus said. "Did Cap Central's initials make you want to come here?"

Cecilia got serious. "No, we had to move when—"

Right then, Marcus's phone chirped. Marcus groaned. "Sorry," he said. "Bad timing." He pulled the phone out of his pocket. He read the text message. "Some people are meeting up on the hill and then going to Primo's for a pizza," he said. "Want to come?"

"What hill?" Cecilia asked.

"You've never been to the hill?" Marcus asked in mock horror. "The hill is that area behind the school."

"So?" Cecilia asked quizzically.

"So it's where Cap Central kids hang out. You can look out over D.C. from there."

"Who's going?" Cecilia asked.

"Joss White, Eva Morales, Carlos, Ferg … that crowd," Marcus said.

"I don't know them," Cecilia said.

"Then it's time you met them," Marcus said, standing up. "You need to meet some nice Cap Central peeps. Besides me, of course. Who you like a lot."

Cecilia punched him playfully. "You're trippin'," she said. "I never said that. But let me tell my mom I'm leaving."

She went inside. In a few minutes, she came back out with her mother. She introduced her to Marcus. After a few minutes of conversation, Marcus and Cecilia left to walk to the school.

When Marcus got home that night, he felt the way he did when he had won a race. He had never met a girl he could talk to as easily as he could talk to Cecilia. She felt the way he did about so many things. Something was starting between them. It made him very happy.

CHAPTER 7

CECILIA

Cecilia had been telling the truth. She did like Marcus. A lot.

And she liked him even more after spending Saturday evening with him.

They had walked to the hill, where he introduced her to his friends.

"Hey, I know you," Joss White said. "Aren't you in my chemistry class with Ms. Phelan?"

"I am," Cecilia said. "I'm the one who has no clue what she's talking about."

"No, I'm the one totally lost." Joss laughed. "She's a good teacher, but that stuff is really hard."

"That's what you get for being so smart," Eva said. "Instead of taking earth sciences like me and Ferg."

"You're on the step team, right?" Joss asked.

Cecilia grimaced involuntarily. Then she nodded.

"We're Poms," Eva said, referring to the school's new pom-pom team. "We're just getting started. You guys are so good. You make us look like clowns."

"And speaking of clowns," Joss said.

Ferg was trying to stand on his head. His extra weight, and the slope of the hill, made him keep tipping over.

"Anybody want Ferg?" Eva said with a laugh. "I'm done with him."

Two more couples joined them. Marcus introduced her to Rainie Burkette and Durand Butler, and Neecy Bethune and Charlie Ray.

Charlie brought a football, and they tossed it around lazily.

"You're the great artist in Ms. Ross's class," Neecy said. "Don't you just love that class?"

"I do," Cecilia agreed. "It's very relaxing. Focusing on drawing makes me forget everything else going on."

"So how long have you and Marcus ..." Neecy asked, her voice trailing off.

"Uh, about an hour?" Cecilia laughed. "Actually, we're just neighbors."

"How nice of him to be so neighborly," Joss joked. "And how very convenient!"

Cecilia joined in the girls' laughter. She felt comfortable with the group. She really liked them. After they all ate, Marcus walked her home.

"Still hate the school?" he asked, putting his arm around her.

"Not as much," Cecilia said. "Your friends are nice."

"There are lots of good people here," Marcus said. "They might not be the people you notice right away. But they're here. And they don't pick on kids who can't defend themselves."

Cecilia knew he meant Remy. For a moment, the now-familiar feelings of disgust washed over her.

But then Marcus kissed her.

All other thoughts went out of her head.

When she pulled away, Marcus was smiling.

"This place has the friendliest neighbors," Cecilia teased.

"You think that was friendly? Wait till

you see what we do at our block parties," Marcus joked.

"This was fun," Cecilia said. "I'm glad you came over."

"I told you, I like your porch swing," Marcus said.

"Yeah, well, it likes you too," Cecilia said.

"See, there it is again," Marcus said. "That liking me part."

"Not me, genius. The swing. I said the swing likes you."

"I am a genius," Marcus said. "It's a swing. It doesn't have feelings,"

"You're insane," Cecilia said. "Good night!"

She walked into her house and locked the door behind her. It had been the happiest night she could remember.

CHAPTER 8

MARCUS

On Tuesday the cross-country team practiced for their upcoming meet. Marcus was looking forward to it. He was in the best shape of his young life.

Marcus knew he wouldn't come in first place. At this point, the rest of the team just tried to improve their own times. Remy's times were spectacular enough that Cap Central won every meet.

Marcus had hoped that running might help get him some scholarship money for college. He knew the college scouts were all focused on Remy. But it would be nice if some of their attention spilled over his way.

When practice was over, Marcus headed for the boys' locker room. Remy Stevenson was standing outside of the girls' locker room. He looked like he was waiting for someone.

"Remy? You okay?" Marcus asked.

Remy nodded.

Something didn't look right. "Why are you waiting there?" Marcus asked.

"Just waiting," Remy said.

Just then, the door to the girls' locker room opened. Thomas Porter walked out. He wore a huge grin. He walked over to Remy and gave him a play punch on the arm. "What's the haps, Remy, my man?" he said.

Remy didn't say anything. He just continued to stand there.

From inside the locker room, Marcus could hear raised voices. It sounded like some girls were fighting. "They need help in there?" he asked Thomas.

"Nah. They're okay," Thomas said. "Fightin' over me! But you know how that is, don't you, stud?" he said to Remy.

Remy still didn't respond.

"Yeah, whatever," Thomas said with a mean laugh. "Later!" He walked off.

The voices coming from the girls' locker room died down. Remy stayed put.

"Remy, you should leave," Marcus said.

"I'm waiting," Remy said again.

"Look, dude, Brennay's seeing Thomas these days," Marcus said harshly. "I don't want to make you feel bad, but they're sort of a thing. She's not a nice girl, man. She's playing with you."

Remy didn't move. Marcus shook his head in frustration. He went into the boys' locker room. From behind him, he heard the door to the girls' locker room open. He didn't bother turning to see who was coming out.

CECILIA

Cecilia couldn't believe it had happened again. Brennay had seen her with Thomas Porter. It wasn't her fault, but Brennay only believed what she saw.

As soon as practice was over, Cecilia had hurried inside the school. She wanted to get to Crossroads. The festival committee was meeting. She wanted to share her plans for the games she would be running.

She went in the door closest to the football field and turned the corner toward the girls' locker room.

Thomas Porter was leaning against the wall. "I been waiting for you," he said, stepping toward her.

Cecilia looked around. She felt nervous. And a little scared. There was no one else in sight.

"Thomas, get out of my way," Cecilia said. "You got me in enough trouble with Brennay the last time."

"Don't worry about Brennay," Thomas said. "She's cool."

"No, she's not!" Cecilia said. "Please, let me get by. You need to leave me alone."

She tried to push past him. He moved to block the door to the locker room.

"She knows I do what I want," Thomas said. "Anyways, I saw you looking at me down on the field. You knew I was waiting for you here, didn't you?"

"You're trippin'," Cecilia said. "I didn't even see you. Now get out of my way!"

Thomas held open the door. Cecilia darted through. When she turned around, he was standing in the locker room, leaning against the door.

"Thomas, are you crazy? Get out of here," Cecilia said. "You can't be in here!"

"One kiss and I'm gone," Thomas said. "Promise."

"Get. Out. Now!" Cecilia said.

He backed her up against the lockers and leaned forward to kiss her. Cecilia put her hands on his shoulders to push him back. Just then, the door to the locker room opened. Brennay walked in, followed by the rest of the step team. Brennay looked from Thomas to Cecilia. Her mouth was open in surprise. The rest of the girls grew quiet.

"There you are!" Thomas said, pulling away. "Good thing you showed up. She pulled me in here," he said, motioning toward Cecilia.

"Seriously?" Brennay said to Cecilia. "*Seriously?*"

"Brennay, no!" Cecilia cried. "He pushed me in here, and I was trying—"

"Hey, I'm out of here!" Thomas said as he pushed through the door. "Though I'm tempted to stay and watch the cat fight."

Cecilia was scared. Brennay was tough, and she was angry. She knew the safest thing would be to get her book bag and leave. She would try to reason with Brennay when she had cooled down.

In an instant, someone grabbed her hair hard enough to pull her head back. Her braids spilled out of the elastic holding them. She whirled around. Brennay slammed her against the lockers, bringing tears to Cecilia's eyes. The look on her face was one of pure rage.

"He's mine!" she screamed. "Mine!"

"I didn't—" Cecilia said, holding up her hands to protect herself.

Brennay just kept screaming. Her face so close to Cecilia's that Cecilia could feel spit landing on her.

From behind Brennay, other girls were getting involved. Brennay's friends were joining in the yelling. Others were trying to calm everyone down. Cecilia just stood where she was. She put her hands over her face. She wasn't going to fight. She just wanted it to be over.

Finally, Brennay stopped to take a breath. "Get out," she ordered. "You got some learning to do about the way we do things here at Cap Central."

Cecilia picked up her book bag. She glanced around for the elastic for her hair. She couldn't see it. She looked at the other team members. Everyone seemed uncomfortable. No one would meet her eye.

"I didn't," she started. "This is just wrong.

Look, Brennay, let's just put an end to this. I quit. Okay?"

"Oh no you don't. You don't get to walk away from this," Brennay said. "I'm the captain of this team. You don't get to quit till you've paid the price. Now just go."

Cecilia shook her head. "Sorry," she whispered. She walked toward the locker room door.

"Just so you know, we decide your punishment," Brennay called out after her. "You'll be hearing from us."

Cecilia opened the door. She almost ran into Remy Stevenson. He was standing just outside the girls' locker room, partly blocking the door. She could see the door to the boys' locker room closing behind whoever had just gone in.

"Remy, go home," Cecilia said. "Just get out of here."

Remy didn't move.

Cecilia stepped around him. Tears filled her eyes. She had never felt more miserable. She wished she'd never come to Cap Central.

CHAPTER 10

MARCUS

Marcus put his tray down on the usual table in the cafeteria. He was the first to arrive. He looked over and saw that once again, Remy was sitting with the step team. Marcus shook his head in disgust.

He felt frustrated that he couldn't do more to help Remy. The problem was, Remy didn't want help. He truly believed Brennay liked him. It was a dilemma. Marcus didn't know how to protect someone who didn't want protecting. Or who even knew he was being bullied.

From the front of the cafeteria, Mrs. Hess tapped on the microphone a few times to get everyone's attention. Friday evening, Cap Central's football team would play Wilson High

School. It was the biggest game of the year. It was the game that drew the biggest crowds. The principal got the lunch crowd cheering as she urged them all to go to the game and support the team.

When she was done, she walked over to the table where the step team sat. Someone got up, and Mrs. Hess sat down beside Brennay. She spoke to the girls, and they all laughed at something she said. Mrs. Hess opened a lunch bag and started to eat. Remy continued to sit on Brennay's other side. He stared at his tray.

"You look like a guy who's having a bad day," Neecy Bethune said, sitting down beside Marcus. "You okay?"

Marcus shook his head. "Just trying to figure out how to protect Remy Stevenson from Brennay," Marcus said. "It's not right, what she's doing to him. But the few times I've tried talking to him, he won't believe it."

Charlie Ray sat down. "What are you guys looking at?" he asked, looking back in the direction of the table with the step team. "Wait. Is that Mrs. Hess eating with the Stepperz?" he asked.

Neecy nodded. "They seem to be her favorites these days. She's having the team participate in more and more activities around here. And I suppose the publicity they get makes the school look good. They've become pretty famous."

"I've never seen her actually eat lunch down here before," Marcus said. "She must like Brennay and the other girls a lot."

"Some of those girls are actually pretty nice," Neecy said. "Marcella Ortiz, Valeria Pincus, and a couple of others. The team is really, really good. They add a lot of spirit to our games. It's a shame Brennay and Zakia hold so much power."

Joss and Eva sat down. "You guys look like you're talking about something serious," Joss said. "Is this private?"

"No, just the usual. We're watching the Stepperz and Remy," Marcus said. "But today's twist is that Mrs. Hess has joined them."

"Do you think she knows about the Remy Points game?" Eva asked.

"She must. Everyone else in the school does," Marcus said. "But she's obviously not stopping it."

"I wish we could think of something,"

Joss said. "There were new points added last night."

"I'm about ready to tell Remy's parents what's going on," Marcus said. "I'll bet they would want to know."

"Hey, what's the plan for Friday night?" Ferg asked, putting down his tray. "We're all going to the game, right?"

"Wouldn't miss it," Neecy said. "It would be nice to win for a change!"

"You guys talking about the game?" Carlos asked, sitting down. "We're all going, right?"

"Well, we are," Eva said proudly. "We are the world-famous Poms, you know. We even get to ride on the team bus."

"I guess you got told," Ferg said to Carlos. "Somehow, we'll have to manage without our girls that night. The girl you were with last week, she's a Stepperz, right?" he asked Marcus. "What was her name? Cicily? Cordelia?"

"Cecilia," Eva said, shaking her head. "Honestly, Ferg, sometimes you make me look like a genius. And, yes, she's on the step team."

"So you want to go to the game with us?" Ferg asked.

"Sure," Marcus said. "What time do you ..." he stopped talking. He saw the whole step team get up from the table where they had been sitting. He tried to find Cecilia among the other girls.

"Want to go? Oh, I don't know. Maybe midnight or one in the morning," Ferg joked.

Marcus stood up to get a better view. He didn't see Cecilia anywhere. He didn't even register what Ferg had said.

"Great. See you then," Marcus said, getting up from the table.

"What was that about?" he heard Eva ask as he walked away.

Marcus didn't wait to hear the answer. He walked quickly to where the step team was leaving the cafeteria. He caught up to Marcella Ortiz, who was at the end of the group.

"Hey, do you know where Cecilia Calhoun is?" he asked her.

Marcella looked uncomfortable. "Why?" she asked, sounding alarmed. "What happened?"

Marcus was perplexed by her response. "What happened?" he repeated in a questioning tone. "Nothing. I was just wondering where she was."

"Well, I don't know. I haven't seen her."

Marcella said. "But if you see her, tell her"—she stopped—"Never mind," she said.

"You all right?" he asked.

"Yeah, fine," Marcella answered. "Hey, I gotta go. Hope you find her."

Marcus watched her walk away. He wondered what was going on.

CHAPTER 11

CECILIA

The next day was torture. Cecilia braced herself for some sort of retribution from Brennay. She deliberately avoided all the places where she had previously socialized with the step team. She didn't even go to the cafeteria for lunch.

As the day wore on, her tension increased. She knew Brennay had something planned. She just didn't know what it was.

That evening, Zakia Johnson called. Her voice was sweet and friendly. She said Brennay felt that she had been too harsh with Cecilia. Brennay had asked Zakia to call. Zakia said Cecilia could quit the team if she really wanted to, but she and Brennay hoped she would stay. The step team's choreography included Cecilia.

They didn't want to have to alter their routines in the middle of the season.

Zakia also invited Cecilia to spend the night with the team at Brennay's apartment after the game. She dropped her voice a bit. Then Zakia said Brennay felt bad about how she had reacted and wanted to be friends.

Zakia said Brennay was having some issues at home, and that her stress about her family problems had caused her reaction. Zakia felt terrible for Brennay. She asked Cecilia to be a friend to her.

Cecilia absolutely did not want to spend the night. She didn't want to be unkind, but she didn't trust Brennay or Zakia. When she hesitated, Zakia proposed a compromise. She asked Cecilia to wait to make a decision about quitting the team until after Friday's game with Wilson High School.

Then Zakia asked Cecilia to perform at the game and spend the night with the team at Brennay's afterward. If Cecilia still wanted to quit, she could do so then. There would be no hard feelings.

Cecilia thought it was a reasonable solution.

Almost too reasonable. It just didn't sound like something Brennay would have decided. Cecilia didn't believe Brennay had had a change of heart. But she didn't want to wreck the routines for the team. Reluctantly, she agreed to perform. Zakia then practically begged Cecilia to also spend the night.

Cecilia felt trapped. Something about the phone call sounded fake. Zakia was just too sweet. It was odd that she would confide her worries about Brennay to Cecilia. Cecilia knew she should say no, but Zakia was too persistent. Finally, she agreed.

When she got off the phone, she immediately regretted having said yes. Her heart told her something was up. She just didn't know what it was. She decided to go along with the plan. But she told herself she would leave the moment something didn't seem right. Even that didn't make her feel better, but at least it was a strategy.

She then asked her mother for permission. Her mother agreed. She said since Cecilia wouldn't be home, she would visit friends in Virginia and stay over. Cecilia's heart fell at the news. With her mother gone, it would be harder for her to ditch the sleepover if something went wrong. She thought about changing her mind, but her mother was so excited about her evening out with friends. Cecilia felt trapped.

On Friday, the whole school was buzzing with excitement about the game with Wilson. Wilson High School had always been Cap Central's main rival. Students from Wilson were richer than the Cap Central kids. They had better equipment and practice facilities. Cap Central's football team was good this year. For the first time in a while, they had a decent chance of beating Wilson.

After school, Cecilia dressed for the game. She put on her uniform and pulled her braids back into a ponytail. She looked for her CC hair elastic. Then she remembered she had lost it in the locker room when Brennay had pulled her hair. She secured her hair with another elastic. Then she tied a blue ribbon accented with big white stars that the Stepperz, cheerleaders, and Poms wore.

There was a knock at her door, and her

mother came in. "Have fun tonight, baby," her mother said. "Big night for Cap Central!"

"Yup," Cecilia said unenthusiastically.

"What's the matter?" her mother asked, surprised. "I thought this was the biggest game of the year."

"It is," Cecilia said. "I'm just having second thoughts about the step team. The other girls are … they're not … they're just not very nice," she said. "In fact, they're kind of mean."

"To you?" her mother asked.

"Mostly to other people," Cecilia said. "I just don't like them much."

"So quit," her mother suggested.

"I may," Cecilia said. "I agreed to at least stick it out through tonight."

"Well, be careful," her mother said. "You know the right thing to do, and you know when something is wrong. These sound like girls who might get the two confused. Don't get pulled into their drama."

"I won't," Cecilia said, sounding more confident than she felt. "I just wish …" It wasn't her mother's fault that Cecilia could no longer attend the private school where she'd gone since kindergarten. Since her father had died, money had been tight.

"I know, baby," her mother said, reading her mind. "I do too."

Tears came to Cecilia's eyes. She still missed her father so much. That was why she had "RIP Daddy" tattooed on her shoulder. No one could see it, but she knew it was there. It was sort of like having him close-by.

Her mother gave her a hug. "It'll get better," she said. "It's about got to, right?"

Cecilia sniffed. "I keep waiting," she said.

"Me too," her mother said with a sad smile. "But we'll get through. I promise, okay? Now, have fun tonight. Remember to use good judgment. And try to have fun. Look for someone on the team who isn't joining in when the others are being mean. That's the person to be friends with. And when I get back from Virginia tomorrow, I want to hear all about it. Now go. Beat Wilson!"

"Rah, rah," Cecilia said sarcastically.

Cecilia kissed her mother goodbye and walked to Cap Central. She joined the rest of the step team in the parking lot. Buses were waiting to take the football team, Stepperz, Poms, cheerleaders, and students over to Wilson. Before everyone boarded, the cheerleaders led the crowd in a few cheers. The step team did a quick routine. They then got on the buses to go to Wilson.

Cecilia sat near the back of one of the buses. She could see Brennay and Zakia sitting several rows ahead of her. Brennay's hair had been fairly short, but she must have gotten it braided with extensions. She had pulled the braids back and secured them with the blue bow. Brennay's hair was now almost as long as Cecilia's. It was secured the same way. From behind, Brennay didn't even look like herself.

The rest of the team was friendly, but no one really sought Cecilia out. She shared a seat with Joss White, whom she had met on the hill the night she was with Marcus. She was glad she had gotten to know Joss and Eva. They were very friendly.

The game was close, but Wilson won. When the buses returned to Cap Central, the girls

collected their gear and headed toward Brennay's apartment.

Brennay had lots of snacks and soft drinks.
Cecilia poured a Coke into a red plastic cup. She
just wanted to get through the night without
crossing Brennay.

After a while, someone knocked at the door.
Brennay opened it, and Remy Stevenson came in.

"Hey, everyone, look who's here," Brennay
said in a falsely cheerful voice. "It's our mascot.
And I think it's picture time. Gather around
Remy and smile!"

The girls grouped around Remy. Cecilia
stayed on the end. She hoped she wouldn't be in
the shot.

After taking a few pictures, Brennay put
down her phone. "This isn't working for me,"
she said. "We need a better backdrop. Come on.
Let's go over to the Trinidad fountain and shoot
some video."

Cecilia looked around at the others. Some
looked as reluctant as she felt. "You sure we
aren't going to get in trouble for leaving your
place?" Marcella Ortiz asked timidly.

"I'll tell my mother we're going out for

pizza," Brennay said. "She believes everything I tell her."

"What about the police?" Valeria Pincus asked. "They won't let us in the park after dark."

"Look at us," Brennay said brightly. "We're the world-famous Stepperz, in our uniforms, taking pictures in front of a fountain. They'll tell us to leave, but they're not going to arrest us. We're too cute."

Cecilia had a very bad feeling about this. She looked around. She could see that some of the other girls were reluctant too. "Brennay, I'm not sure this is a good idea," Cecilia said. "It's dark out. Let's just take pictures here."

Brennay flashed her a look of pure hatred. In a super-sweet voice that contrasted with her expression, she said, "Thanks so much, Cecilia, but you no longer have a vote." She looked around the room. "Anybody else? Anybody else think they don't have to do what the captain of this team tells them to do?"

The rest of the girls were quiet.

"Didn't think so," Brennay said. "All right, let's go to the park."

They walked out of the apartment. No

one walked with Cecilia. She had never felt so alone. They strolled to the small park on Morse Street.

Brennay turned to the team. "Line up in front of the fountain."

The girls got into formation. Brennay handed her phone to Remy and asked him to take a picture. After a few shots, she got out of line and took the phone. She reached up to hug Remy. Cecilia could see her whisper something to him. He nodded, but he didn't look happy.

Brennay turned back to face the team. "You all know Remy is the best mascot any team could have, right?"

All the girls murmured their agreement.

"Well, you might not know that he's also a superhero," Brennay said. "You've got to watch this!" She turned to Zakia. "Z, you ready to film?" she asked.

Zakia held her phone in front of her. "Ready," she said.

"Count of three, Remy," Brennay said. "One, two, three!" She tossed her phone. Remy flew toward it. He grabbed it before it fell on the ground.

"Did you get it?" Brennay asked.

"Not sure," Zakia said. "It's dark. Try it again."

Brennay held out the phone. "One, two, three!" she said. She threw the phone, and again Remy ran hard to catch it. He brought it back to her.

"One more time," Brennay said cheerfully. "You are so awesomely fast. Ready?"

Remy nodded.

This time, Brennay tossed the phone in the direction of the fountain. "Whoops!" she said sarcastically.

Remy leapt over the side, but not in time to catch the phone as it fell into the water. Remy grabbed for it, but he stumbled and lost his footing. He went down. He came up holding the phone. He climbed out of the fountain. It was a cool night, and he was shivering.

"Oh, Remy, you're my hero," Brennay said.

Remy handed over the phone.

"I missed it," Zakia said. "Let's do it again."

Remy was shaking uncontrollably. Cecilia realized he was crying. She couldn't stand it. She put her arms around him to warm him up. "Remy, you don't have to do this," she said.

He stood stiffly, still shaking hard.

Cecilia turned toward Brennay. She felt hot with anger. She no longer cared what Brennay thought about her. This was wrong.

"This stops now, Brennay," Cecilia said coldly. "No more."

She turned back toward Remy. "Go home, Remy. Before you catch pneumonia."

He didn't move. His head was down and his body shook. But he didn't make a move to leave.

"I think it's time you went home, Calhoun," Brennay said. "Remy doesn't mind. Any of this. He likes it."

Cecilia had no idea what Remy thought about Brennay's treatment of him. But she knew it didn't matter.

"Brennay, what you're doing is wrong. And I won't be a part of it. He deserves better." She turned to Remy. "Remy, you don't have to take this. Any of it. Brennay's not your friend, no matter what she says. She's beyond mean. She's evil."

Remy stood silent.

Cecilia turned back to Brennay. "I'm done," she said. "You can put my stuff on your front porch. I'll get it tomorrow."

She turned to walk out of the park.

"Wait, Cecilia!" someone said.

Cecilia turned around.

Marcella Ortiz was following her. "I'm coming too."

"Me too," Valeria Pincus said.

Cecilia couldn't believe it. She wasn't the only one who'd had enough.

"Really?" Cecilia said.

The two girls nodded. They all walked together out of the park.

"You know she'll never forgive us for this," Cecilia said as they walked up Morse Street.

Marcella laughed bitterly. "I'd never forgive myself if I'd stayed," she said. "I think she's crazy."

"I've been wanting to walk out for a while," Valeria said. "This was the last straw."

"Meanwhile, my mother is going to kill me

when she learns I'm not staying at Brennay's," Cecilia said. "I'm so glad you guys left with me. I would have hated walking home alone."

"Would you guys like to stay at my house tonight?" Valeria asked. "My parents won't mind."

Cecilia knew her mother would be mad when she heard there had been a change of plans. But she hoped that once she explained the circumstances, her mother would be okay.

"Sure!" she said, feeling almost happy.

CHAPTER 12

MARCUS

Saturday afternoon, Marcus went to the recreation center to play a little basketball. Ferg and Carlos were there. Soon they were joined by Durand Butler and Charlie Ray.

Something seemed off. It was fun, but the other guys were acting a little formal with him. Finally, he'd had enough. He grabbed the ball and said, "Okay, what is with you guys? You're all acting so strange."

Carlos and Ferg looked at each other. Durand looked at the ground. Then he looked up at Marcus. "It's that thing with Cecilia Calhoun," he said. "Sorry, man. I know you liked her."

Marcus went cold. "What happened to her?" he asked urgently.

The other guys looked uncomfortably at

each other. "You didn't see *Cap Central Chatter* this morning, did you?" Carlos asked.

"Obviously not," Marcus said sharply. "So tell me. What's happened."

"She's apparently the winner of the Remy Points game," Ferg said. "There are lots of pictures of her with him. Sorry, man. I think she had us all fooled."

Marcus couldn't believe it. But the others seemed convinced. Since he hadn't seen the blog, he didn't know what to say.

"Whatever," he answered finally, tossing the basketball to Durand. "I'll see you later."

He walked back home to check the *Chatter*. He couldn't believe what the guys had said. He knew Cecilia. She wouldn't be a part of something like that.

He went into his house and flipped on his computer. Then he accessed the blog. He couldn't believe what he saw.

"WE HAVE A WINNER!" the headline screamed. It went on to say that Cecilia Calhoun, former member of the Stepperz, had scored the highest number of Remy Points for what she did with Remy Stevenson over the weekend.

And there were pictures.

Cecilia kissing Remy.

Cecilia with her arms around Remy.

And the worst one: Cecilia lying on top of Remy, wearing only a sports bra and gym shorts. Her face was shadowed, but she was clearly recognizable. Her CC elastic was holding back her long braids.

Marcus felt like he'd been punched in the stomach. No wonder the guys felt so awkward around him.

Cecilia was no better than Brennay Baxter. In fact, she was worse. He didn't know what was going on in that last picture, but he could imagine. He couldn't believe he'd been so totally wrong about her. She had put on such an act about doing the right thing and standing up to anyone who was being cruel.

But clearly it was all talk.

He felt so embarrassed. He had fallen for her act. He briefly wondered why the blog described her as a "former member of the Stepperz." All he could hope was that the team had decided her behavior toward Remy was more than they would tolerate.

He thought for a moment about what he should do. Then he pasted the web address of the blog into an email and sent it to Mrs. Hess. If the principal didn't know about the blog already, it was time she learned what was being done to a Cap Central student.

Marcus also decided that the next time he saw Remy's parents, he would tell them how their son was being taken advantage of. He knew his action was long overdue. Had he done the right thing earlier, whatever went down that weekend wouldn't have happened.

But it needed to stop, and even if he was late in acting, he would do all he could to protect Remy now.

Most of all? He knew he would never, ever speak to Cecilia again.

CHAPTER 13

CECILIA

Cecilia enjoyed the sleepover with Marcella and Valeria. It was the first time since transferring to Cap Central that she felt she might have some girlfriends. In the morning, she walked home. She wanted to be there to explain why she wasn't at Brennay's apartment.

When she got home, she turned on her computer. Even though she hated reading the *Chatter* blog, she opened it anyway.

She felt like her heart stopped beating.

There she was, declared the winner of the Remy Points competition.

A picture of her holding a red plastic drink cup: 5 points

A picture of her with her arms around Remy: 25 points

A picture of her kissing Remy: 75 points

A picture of someone who looked like her, wearing her CC hair elastic, lying on top of Remy: 200 points

She wanted to die.

Brennay had her revenge. The whole school would think Cecilia had taken advantage of Remy.

The first picture made it look as if she were drinking alcohol at a party. The next two pictures were clear shots of her face. And the last one—the worst one—was shadowy enough to shield whoever it was from being identified.

The hair on the girl in the picture wasn't as long as Cecilia's. But no one else besides Cecilia would realize that. The braids and the hair elastic would be enough to convince most people that it was Cecilia lying on top of Remy while wearing skimpy clothes.

Cecilia fell back onto her bed. She stared at the ceiling. She knew she was in deep, deep trouble. The pictures implied that more than kissing might have been going on. It looked like she was abusing Remy. Even though Remy didn't look as if he minded the kissing in the last picture, Cecilia suspected the school would consider it some sort of bullying. Especially since Remy was autistic.

Her mother knocked at the door.

"Hi, baby. I'm home. How was your evening?" her mother said, walking into the room. She stopped short when she saw Cecilia. "Honey, what's wrong?" she asked in alarm.

"Oh, Mom, I'm in trouble," Cecilia said. "I think I messed up big-time."

Her mother's eyes got wide. "What did you do?" she asked, sounding angry. "Tell me."

So Cecilia told her everything.

How Brennay had Remy attend step team functions.

How Brennay had made Remy the mascot and made all the girls kiss him.

How *Cap Central Chatter* started awarding Remy Points.

How Brennay made him fetch her phone Friday night, but then she deliberately threw it into the fountain.

How she posed someone on top of Remy using Cecilia's lost hair elastic.

Cecilia's mother shook her head in disbelief.

"Why you, though?" she asked. "What does she have against you?"

So Cecilia told her about her two interactions with Thomas Porter, and how Brennay wouldn't believe she was innocent.

"Wow," her mother said finally. "That girl is bad news. Okay, let's figure out where we go from here. But first you have to tell me with absolute honesty, is everything you just told me the truth? Did you mess with that poor boy in any other way except for the kiss and trying to help him last night?"

"That's all," Cecilia said. "I swear it."

"All right. On Monday we're going to Mrs. Hess. You're going to have to tell her what happened."

"Oh, Mom," Cecilia said. "I can't! The whole school will hate me. You have no idea how popular—and powerful—Brennay is. My life at Cap Central will be over."

"Do you see any other way out?" her mother asked. "I understand how you feel, but—"

"You have no idea how I feel," Cecilia said in a small voice. She felt worse than she had ever felt in her life.

"I'm sorry, baby," her mother said softly. "But

at this point, I think it's high time you did the right thing."

Cecilia rolled over and buried her face in her pillow. "Can you leave me alone for a while so I can think?" she asked

She felt her mother kiss the top of her head. "Of course. We can talk about this tomorrow."

Cecilia heard the click of the door closing. At that point, the tears came.

CHAPTER 14

MARCUS

Marcus was so angry with Cecilia. He felt betrayed. She had lied to him by pretending to be one kind of person, when really she was just the opposite.

He wanted the step team to quit messing with Remy. Problem was, Remy didn't want the attention to stop. Marcus didn't even know how Remy felt about the pictures. It was possible that he liked whatever he and Cecilia had been doing in the last photo.

But Marcus felt like the rest of the school had a responsibility to help a classmate. They had to do something. He just didn't know what.

He picked up the phone and called Keisha Jackson. Keisha was president of the student government association. She was always looking for ways that Capital Central kids could serve the D.C. community.

"Did you see today's *Chatter*?" he asked her.

"Yeah," Keisha said. "It made me sick. I can't believe what that new girl did with Remy."

"Me too," Marcus said bitterly. "And I've been thinking about it. There are some programs that need volunteers. Programs to help kids with special needs. I think we should get Cap Cent kids to participate."

"You mean like the Special Olympics?" Keisha asked.

"Yeah, but there are others," Marcus said. "The Best Buddies program is one. Student athletes pair up with special needs kids and help them. Encourage them in sports."

"I really like that idea," Keisha said. "I'll bet there are enough people who feel guilty about not helping Remy. We could get lots of volunteers. Could you make some calls?"

Marcus said he would. It wasn't enough to make him feel better over dropping the ball with Remy. But it would help.

CHAPTER 15

CECILIA

Something very bad has happened that concerns a student at Capital Central. You may already have received information about this. I would appreciate meeting with you first thing on Monday to tell you the truth.

Cecilia read over the email several times, and then signed her name. She pressed send.

She opened her bedroom door and saw that her mother was already up. "You couldn't sleep either I guess," she said.

"Not really," her mother said. "Listen, I've been thinking, and I think you need to—"

"Mom, wait," Cecilia said, holding up her hand. "I've already done something. I wrote to Mrs. Hess and told her I need to meet with her first thing tomorrow. I hope I can meet with her before she sees the blog. But in any case, I need to tell her what Brennay has been doing to Remy. The problem is, it's going to look as if I'm just trying to shift the blame. But I can't help that. I'm going to tell her everything."

"Oh, honey, you are so brave," her mother said with tears in her eyes. "I'm so proud of you."

"Just out of curiosity, what were you going to tell me to do?" Cecilia asked.

"I was all set to try to convince you to do exactly what you are going to do. I should have had faith that you would do the right thing without me forcing you," her mom said.

"You know, life for me at Cap Central is over at this point," Cecilia said. "Everyone's going to hate me, and they'll all believe the worst. I'm not sure I can ... I don't think I can go back to school after this." She felt her eyes fill up with hot tears.

"You're not going to drop out," her mother said in horror.

"I doubt they're going to let me stay after this," Cecilia said hotly. "But even if they do, my life at Cap Cent is done. I can't spend the rest of high school surrounded by people who think I'm the kind of person who would take advantage of someone with autism."

"Let's take it one step at a time," her mother said. "Sometimes people are better than you expect."

"One other thing I have to do," Cecilia said.

Her mother looked at her expectantly.

"I've got to tell Mrs. Reynolds at Crossroads about this," Cecilia said. "I need to tell her before someone else does."

"You're right, of course," her mother said. "I'm sorry, baby. I know working there means a lot to you."

"Do you think she'll make me quit?" Cecilia asked, almost in tears again.

"I truly don't know," her mother answered. "But you should be prepared for that possibility. Her responsibility is to the kids who go to Crossroads. She may think it will make parents uncomfortable if they knew about this thing with Remy."

Cecilia buried her face in her hands. "Then I'll never be able to work with special needs kids," she said. "This will always be out there, even though it's not true."

"Remember, Cecilia, one step at a time," her mother said. "You've got enough on your plate without looking down the road at your whole adult career."

"Will you come with me tomorrow when I talk to Mrs. Hess?" Cecilia asked.

"Of course," her mother answered. "From everything you've told me, though, she sounds like a reasonable person. Let's assume she's going to have an open mind about this."

"She's going to see pictures of me half-naked, lying on top of a kid with special needs," Cecilia said with disgust. "If you were Remy's mother, how reasonable would you want Mrs. Hess to be?"

Her mother was quiet. "I'd want whoever was responsible to be forced to do community service, working with people who are challenged in some way. But that's Brennay, not you."

"Right," Cecilia said. "And you're the only one who is going to believe that."

"I do believe it, baby. You're a good girl. Don't forget that."

"I messed up big, didn't I?" Cecilia said, the tears coming back.

"Honey, everybody messes up. Everybody. Messing up is just a part of life. It's how you deal with whatever happens afterward that says what kind of person you are.

"Good people admit their mistakes and try to make them right. Bad people lie, cheat, and pull others down in order to hide their rottenness from the world.

"Yeah, you messed up. But you're trying to make it right. And in my heart, I have to believe that your goodness will protect you."

She leaned over and kissed Cecilia on the forehead.

"You're my good girl, and I have faith in you," she said. "Now try not to worry."

CHAPTER 16

MARCUS

Marcus was glad he had sent the blog link to Mrs. Hess. And he felt good about the idea of starting a Best Buddies program at Cap Central. But he wanted to do more to help Remy.

Remy's autism prevented him from recognizing what Brennay was doing. But Marcus could see it for what it was: bullying. Remy wouldn't listen when Marcus tried to help him. It was time his parents were told.

Marcus knew Remy often ran on the Cap Central track on Sunday afternoons. His parents usually sat in the stands and read while Remy ran. He left his house and headed for the school. As he walked past Cecilia's house, he saw she was on her porch swing. He didn't want to talk to her. He kept walking.

He was almost past her house when she called out to him.

"Hey, Marcus," she called.

He didn't stop.

"Marcus?" she said louder. "Please. Wait a minute."

Marcus waited while Cecilia walked up to him.

"Hey," she said.

"What?" he answered coldly.

"Marcus, those pictures weren't me. At least, they weren't what they looked like. I didn't do those things. The most I did was kiss Remy for good luck one night. That's all. The rest are fake."

"You are unbelievable," Marcus said with a bitter laugh. "The pictures are fake? The only thing fake about this is you. You and your 'I want to do the right thing' act. I'm just so sorry that I fell for it. You really had me believing you were better than that."

Cecilia felt as if she couldn't breathe. She turned to walk away.

"What I'll never understand is what would make someone—you, anyone—think it was funny to humiliate Remy that way. I've seen how he looks at you step team girls. He idolizes you guys. He trusts you. You obviously took advantage of that trust. And for what? A few laughs?"

Cecilia started to defend herself. Then she stopped. She was crushed that Marcus would so quickly believe the worst about her. "You know what?" she said sharply. "You're right. I'm an awful person. Good for you for figuring it out so quickly."

"That's about the only thing you and I agree on," Marcus said. He turned and walked toward the school.

As he expected, Remy's father was sitting in the stands. Marcus climbed the stairs and sat beside him.

"Hey, Marcus, how're you doing, son?" Mr. Stevenson asked.

"Not great," Marcus answered. "I need to tell you something that concerns Remy."

Mr. Stevenson looked concerned. He put down his newspaper. "Go ahead," he said.

So Marcus told him everything. About *Cap Central Chatter* and the Remy Points game.

About Brennay and how Remy seemed to be infatuated with her. How she led Remy on, making him think she liked him, while making fun of him behind his back. And finally, about the pictures that had been posted of Cecilia kissing Remy, putting her arms around him, and lying on top of him.

Mr. Stevenson looked stunned.

"Why didn't anyone stop this?" he asked. "Why did all of you allow this to happen? You were supposed to be his friend. Or were you just pretending?"

"I tried," Marcus said, sounding lame to himself. "A couple of us did. We tried telling him that Brennay was no good. But he wouldn't listen."

"Did you try telling someone in charge? The coach? The principal? A teacher or guidance counselor?"

Marcus shook his head miserably.

Mr. Stevenson was quiet for a moment. "You know, Remy's mother and I have been worried about him for his whole life, wondering if people were going to take advantage of him because he's not like other kids," he said. "We've tried to teach him to protect himself, but we knew we couldn't—wouldn't—always be there for him. We were so happy when Remy joined the cross-country and track teams. He had always been a runner. It was one of the symptoms of his autism. From the time he could walk, he ran everywhere.

"Joining a team was perfect. He had an outlet for the running, plus we believed the bonds between team members would help protect him when we weren't around." Mr. Stevenson shook his head angrily. "Sounds like we were dead wrong about that last part."

Marcus felt sick. In a way, he was no better than Cecilia. His lack of action was almost as bad as what she had done.

"I appreciate you telling me this," Mr. Stevenson said. "At least you came to me. That's more than anyone else did." He stood up and moved to another seat.

Marcus waited for a moment. He then got up and left. He had never felt so low.

CHAPTER 17

CECILIA

Cecilia checked her email obsessively all day Sunday for a response from Mrs. Hess. It finally came around four. It was a request for Cecilia and her mother to be at the school for a meeting at nine Monday morning.

Cecilia didn't sleep much that night. By morning, she was up and dressed before her mother's alarm even rang. She and her mother arrived at the school fifteen minutes before the scheduled meeting.

As they walked into the building, Cecilia's mother gave her a hug. "This is going to be okay," she said. "I promise."

Cecilia's eyes filled with tears. "I hope you're right," she said.

They walked into the main office. Mrs.

Dominguez, the principal's secretary, asked them to take a seat. As they waited, several people came into the office. Mrs. Dominguez directed each of them into the principal's office.

The phone rang on Mrs. Dominguez's desk. "You may go in now," she said.

They walked into Mrs. Hess's office. Mrs. Hess introduced Cecilia and her mother to Mr. Gable, the school's head security guard, and Ms. Drake, the head of the Special Education Department at Capital Central.

"I think we all know why we're here today," Mrs. Hess began. "Cecilia? Since you emailed me yesterday, I think you should start. I will tell you, however, that I've seen the pictures of you on *Cap Central Chatter*."

"You've seen pictures," Mrs. Calhoun corrected.

"I'm sorry?" Mrs. Hess asked.

"You said you've seen pictures of Cecilia. I'm saying you've seen pictures. There's no proof that they are of my daughter."

"Hey, it's your kid in the shot," Mr. Gable said. "What are you saying, that—"

"Mister Gable, please," Mrs. Hess said. "Let's hear her out."

Cecilia took a deep breath.

She described everything she could remember. Brennay making all the girls kiss Remy. The awarding of Remy Points on *Cap Central Chatter*. Seeing Brennay "borrow" Remy's Wizards sweatshirt. She described how Remy seemed uncomfortable with the attention. She also described how Brennay accused her of being with Thomas Porter.

"And what is your relationship with Thomas?" Mrs. Hess asked.

"I have no relationship with Thomas," Cecilia said hotly. "None. I really, really, dislike the guy."

"Okay, understood," the principal said, shaking her head grimly. "But tell us about this second picture. The one where you have your arms around Remy."

So Cecilia explained what happened at the fountain. About Brennay forcing Remy to fetch her cell phone. About deliberately throwing it into the fountain. She explained how she had finally told Brennay to stop, and that Remy was crying. She said she put her arms around him because he was shivering.

"And then what happened?" Mrs. Hess said. "Tell us the rest of it. How did you end up lying on Remy in the last picture?"

"That's not me," Cecilia said. "I don't know who it is."

Mrs. Hess looked skeptical. "Cecilia, you've been very forthright up until now. You need to tell us the truth. That looks like you. That's your hair elastic, isn't it? Don't you wear a hair orna-ment with CC on it?"

"It's mine, but not me," Cecilia said. "Bren-nay grabbed me in the locker room one day, and my hair elastic flew off. I left without it. I guess Brennay and her friends found it. But I can prove that's not me."

"Really?" Mrs. Hess asked. "Please do."

"Well, if you look closely, you can see those aren't my braids," Cecilia said. "Mine are real. Those are too perfect. They're extensions. Not even very good ones. And the hair is not as long as mine. But that's not all."

Cecilia stood up. She was wearing a tank

top under her sweater. She pulled her sweater off over her head and turned around.

"You have a tattoo," Mrs. Hess whispered.

"Whoever is in that picture doesn't have any ink," Cecilia said. "And I do."

"You have a tattoo?!" Cecilia's mother gasped. "When did you get a tattoo?"

"After Daddy died," Cecilia said. "I wanted it to be between him and me, so I never told you."

"We'll talk about that later," her mother said firmly. "But believe me, I'm thanking you—and your father—for it right now."

"You can put your sweater back on," Mrs. Hess said, her voice sounding kinder. "It's obvious you aren't the girl in the last picture. What happened Friday night after the cell phone incident?"

"I don't know," Cecilia said. "I left."

"Left for where?" her mother said. "You told me you were spending the night at Brennay's!"

"I just couldn't," Cecilia said. "And you weren't home, so I didn't want to go to our place. Marcella Ortiz and Valeria Pincus were also disgusted with the whole thing, and they left with me. We slept over at Valeria's house.

I was going to tell you, but once I saw the pictures, I forgot."

"And that's another thing we'll talk about later," her mother said. "But it sounds like these other two girls can back up what you've told us here, is that right?"

"They should," Cecilia said. "Hopefully, they're not too scared of Brennay. She's pretty powerful around here."

"We'll get them in here today. Cecilia, if everything you've told us checks out, I think you're in the clear. I'm totally disgusted by the behavior of the step team, and how nobody put a stop to it. You could have told any guidance counselor, any teacher, any adult at all," Mrs. Hess said sternly. "Action would have been taken to protect Remy before things got out of hand. Which they clearly did. But I'm going to let you return to class now. That is, until we finish our investigation."

Cecilia stood up. "Thanks, but I'm not going to go back to class," she said. "In fact, I don't think I'm ever coming back here. This is not a nice place. You've got mean girls running the show. They bully vulnerable students. No one tried to stop it until I emailed you myself. This blog has been going on for weeks," Cecilia snapped. "You're right. I didn't tell anyone. Because it sure looked to me like you supported everything the Stepperz did.

"With all due respect, Mrs. Hess, you asked us to perform at every school function, and even some outside of school. You seemed to be best friends with Brennay. You even sat with the step team at lunch and ate with them. If you didn't know about the blog, you should have known about the blog."

Cecilia turned to Ms. Drake. "Remy Stevenson is a champion runner. And no one was looking out for him? I'm not proud of what I did, or what I didn't do. But you all share the blame. Cap Central is about to become famous because of his running. Unfortunately, if this story gets out, you'll also be famous for how he was treated. But I won't be a part of it."

"Cecilia, before you go, let me just say a few things," Mrs. Hess said. "First of all, I want you to know I was unaware of this blog until someone sent it to me on Saturday. Should I have known about it earlier? I wish I had. I only know what people tell me, and I truly wish someone had informed me of the blog and this vicious game before now.

"But in any case, I agree with much of what you said. We all share the blame, and we should have been looking out for Remy. Not just for Remy, but for all our students, particularly those who are challenged in some way. I'm very impressed that you stood up and did something. I wish others had." Mrs. Hess sighed. "You are the kind of student I want to have here at Capital Central. I hope you'll reconsider your decision to leave."

Cecilia and her mother left the office. Cecilia knew she was in trouble for the tattoo and for not telling her mother where she had spent Friday night. But it looked as if she might not be in trouble at school.

CHAPTER 18

MARCUS

Students were talking about the pictures all day Monday. Rumors were flying. Cecilia had been expelled. The police had been brought in. Remy's parents were threatening to sue the school.

By lunchtime, Marcus had had enough. The whole thing was terrible on so many levels. He hated himself for not having done enough to protect Remy when he knew he was being bullied. But he also hated himself for having so badly misjudged Cecilia and fallen for her lies. He was humiliated. What made things worse was that deep down, he still liked her.

He sat at a table in a corner. His back was to the rest of the lunchroom. He didn't want to talk to anyone. He just wanted to be left alone.

"Hey," a voice said from behind him.

He turned around. Joss White was standing there, a sympathetic look on her face.

"Mind if I sit?"

"I'm not very good company, I'm afraid," Marcus said.

"I'm not looking for good company," Joss said, pulling out a chair. "I just wanted to talk to you."

Marcus continued to eat. "Want my cookie?" he asked, pushing his plate toward her.

Joss shook her head and pushed it back. "Look, Marcus, I wanted to tell you that I really liked Cecilia. I know how you must feel—"

"Really, Joss? You know how I feel? The pictures weren't of Carlos, now were they?" Marcus said sarcastically.

"No, they weren't," Joss said softly. "But from what I'm hearing, they weren't of Cecilia either. You've probably been avoiding everyone today, so you don't know what people are saying. But there's a lot of talk about how the last picture ... You know, the worst one. It wasn't even Cecilia. And the picture of her with her arm around Remy was from a time when she was trying to help him. I think you should wait to make a decision about her until you hear the facts."

"From who? I seriously doubt the facts will be published in *Cap Central Chatter*," Marcus said bitterly.

"You could try asking Cecilia," Joss said. "That might be a place to start."

"Yeah, well, I don't think that's going to happen," Marcus said. "That ship has sailed."

"It's not completely out of the harbor," Joss said with a smile. "You should try to wave it down."

Marcus picked up his tray to leave. Joss stood and gave him a hug.

Marcus passed the table where the step team sat. He didn't even look their way. Then Remy walked into the cafeteria. He started toward the step team table.

Marcus headed his way. "Hey, Remy," he said. "Want to sit with me over here?" he asked, motioning to another table.

"I eat with the Stepperz," Remy said.

"But I want to talk to you about the cross-country meet," Marcus lied. "Why don't you sit over here with me?"

"I want to eat with the Stepperz," Remy repeated.

Marcus shook his head in frustration. Even after all that had happened, Remy didn't get it.

"Remy, they aren't your friends," he said. "They're not nice people. You shouldn't be with them."

"They are my friends. You're not nice to say things about them," Remy said. He walked over to the table filled with girls.

Marcus watched for a minute. Then he left the cafeteria. It was all so wrong. But at this point, there truly was nothing more he could do.

CHAPTER 19

CECILIA

Cecilia asked her mother to drop her off at Crossroads. She had to talk to Mrs. Reynolds before she heard the story from someone else.

Mrs. Reynolds was in her office. "Why, Cecilia," she said. "How nice to see you! No school today?"

"Not for me," Cecilia said. "I need to talk to you."

"Go ahead, dear," Mrs. Reynolds said.

Cecilia told her the story. When she was done, Mrs. Reynolds shook her head. "I've never understood cruelty," she said. "Does it make the person feel good to be so mean? How does this Brennay live with herself? She must feel awful about herself. Somehow being mean to someone vulnerable must elevate her in her own eyes. How terrible to go through life that way."

"I can't believe you can feel sympathetic toward her," Cecilia said. "She's rotten through and through. She doesn't deserve your kindness."

"Cecilia, everyone deserves kindness," Mrs. Reynolds said. "I couldn't live with myself if I were mean in exchange. And I know you are kind as well. Which is why I totally believe what you've told me."

"You do?" Cecilia said hopefully. "Can I still work here?"

"If you don't, I think we'll have a mutiny from the little ones you work with," Mrs. Reynolds said, laughing. "But before I give you the go-ahead, I'm going to call your school. I need to talk to the principal. I need to make sure the school's investigation backs up what you've told me. Not because I don't believe you, but because I need to make sure we're all on the same page, in case any parents of Crossroads students hear the story and want to know the facts. I care about you a great deal, but my priorities are the program and its students. Do you understand?"

"I do," Cecilia said. "In the meantime, can I volunteer this week?"

"Why don't you do this," Mrs. Reynolds said. "I'm going to give you all the posters and markers so you can make signs for Saturday's festival. I'll give you a list of what we need. You can work at home. I'll email or call you when I've cleared this with Cap Central."

Cecilia knew it was fair. She just hoped Mrs. Hess would back her up when Mrs. Reynolds called.

MARCUS

Marcus's bedroom door flew open. "Marcus! Marcus! Marcus!" Sammy shouted, jumping on the bed. "We have to go to the festival."

Marcus groaned. It was Saturday, the day he had promised to take Sam to Crossroads.

"It's too early," he moaned, pulling the covers over his head.

"I want to go!" Sammy wailed.

"All right," Marcus said. "But go watch cartoons while I get ready."

Marcus jumped in the shower and got dressed. Then he poured a bowl of cereal. He ate it, trying to avoid looking at Sammy. The little boy was staring at Marcus, as if he were willing his cousin to hurry.

"All right," Marcus said. "Let's go!"

They walked to the Trinidad Recreation Center. Sammy talked non-stop. "First I want to do the bouncy castle. CeCe said I could. She said she would help me get in and out. She said she'd hang out with us today. And I want to do the beanbag toss. You throw them as far as you can. CeCe said she knew I would win. And I want to run in a race. And—"

"And let me guess. The amazing CeCe said you'd be faster than anybody, right?" Marcus laughed. "I can't wait to meet this girl!"

They got near the recreation center. The place was swarming with little kids and their parents. It was a beautiful fall day, with clear blue skies and the golden light that seemed to only happen in autumn.

Marcus signed Sammy in. They put on their name tags. "Okay, Sam, what do you want to do first?" he asked.

"Find CeCe," Sammy said. "And go in the bouncy castle."

They could see the corners of the bouncy house in the distance. They headed that way.

"CeCe," Sammy shrieked. He took off running.

Marcus stopped short.

Sammy ran right up to Cecilia. She opened her arms and hugged Sam. The little boy nearly knocked her over.

Marcus was furious. He didn't understand why she was there. But after what she had done to Remy, there was no way she should be allowed anywhere near the special needs kids who attended Crossroads.

He came nearer.

"Are your mom and dad here?" he heard Cecilia say to Sammy.

"No, my cousin," Sammy said. "Here he is!"

Cecilia looked up. In an instant, her face changed from a smile of welcome to a look of shock.

"CeCe?" he asked.

"My initials," she answered.

"Well, *CC*, take your hands off my cousin. You shouldn't be allowed anywhere near these kids. I want you gone."

"It's not actually up to you," Cecilia said. "But you're welcome to take your concerns to the program director. She's right over there. In the blue shirt." She pointed to Mrs. Reynolds

"Come on, Sammy, we're going over there," Marcus said.

"Nooo," Sammy whined. "I want the bouncy castle. CeCe, will you take me?"

"Apparently, I can't," Cecilia said gently. "Sammy, you need to go with your cousin. I'll just see you later."

"NOOO!" Sammy cried louder.

The other kids and their families were looking their way. Marcus could see Mrs. Reynolds approaching.

"Good morning, Sammy!" Mrs. Reynolds said to the little boy, giving him a hug. "Ready for your fun day?" She held out her hand to Marcus. "I'm Mrs. Reynolds," she said. "Are you Sammy's brother?"

Marcus shook her hand. "I'm his cousin Marcus DiMonte," he said.

"So why is our little guy crying on such a lovely day?" Mrs. Reynolds said.

"Cecilia Calhoun shouldn't be here," Marcus said. "She shouldn't be anywhere near these kids. You probably don't know this, but she ... she's not the person you might think she is."

"Mrs. Reynolds, I can leave," Cecilia said

quickly. "Or I can just make sure I'm nowhere near Sammy."

"No, Cecilia, you're going to stay and do the job you've been assigned to do," Mrs. Reynolds said firmly.

"I want CeCe," Sammy yelled. "You said you'd help me with the bouncy castle."

Marcus felt trapped. He didn't want to upset Sammy, but there was no way he would allow Cecilia anywhere near the little boy.

"Maybe I should just go," Cecilia said.

"No, I'm sorry," Mrs. Reynolds said. "We need you here. I'm insisting that you stay."

"Something you ought to know about *CC* here," Marcus said angrily. "I don't suppose she told you she's under investigation for bullying and abusing a special needs kid at Cap Central."

"Something you ought to know, young man," Mrs. Reynolds said fiercely. "Cecilia is the best volunteer we've ever had. She is kind. And sensitive. And one of the most caring individuals I've ever known. I trust her completely. She already told me about the accusations against her, and I knew immediately they were false.

"But just in case I ran into a family member

who needed reassurance, I called the school. She's been cleared. It's a shame you don't know her better. If you did, you wouldn't have believed the lies being told. I hope you'll learn a lesson from this. Not to believe everything you hear." Mrs. Reynolds held Marcus's gaze.

Marcus couldn't believe the school had cleared Cecilia. He had seen the pictures. "Mrs. Reynolds, I appreciate that you trust her," he said. "But you can't know all of it. I do know Cecilia. Or at least I thought I did," he said. "Bottom line, she doesn't go anywhere near my cousin. She can't even look at him."

"That's up to you," Mrs. Reynolds continued. "You can let your cousin stay here and enjoy his day with a counselor he loves. Or you can ruin it for him by making him leave. Bottom line?" she repeated. "Cecilia stays. Whether you do or not is up to you."

For a moment, no one said anything. Then Sam looked at Marcus. The tears were still wet on his cheeks. "Can we stay, Marcus?" he asked with a sniff. "Please?"

Marcus looked away for a moment. He was torn. "Sure," he said finally. "We can stay."

"Yay!" Sammy said, hugging Cecilia around the legs. "CeCe, did you hear? I can stay!"

"I did hear," Cecilia said. "That's great. Sammy, why don't you and your cousin go over to the bouncy castle? I'll see you later."

"You said you'd play with me today." Sammy looked stricken. "Why won't you go with me? You said you would." He looked like he was about to cry again.

Cecilia looked at Marcus. "Your call," she said.

Marcus knew he'd lost the battle. "For Sammy," he said. "No other reason."

"Don't flatter yourself," Cecilia said dryly. "Of course it's only for Sammy." She turned to the little boy. "Okay, kiddo, I'm staying. What would you like to do now? Bouncy castle? Face painting? Beanbag toss?"

"Face painting," Sammy said. "Can I look like Spiderman?"

Even Marcus laughed at that. "That'll take a lot of paint, buddy," he said. "But let's check it out." He reached down for Sammy's hand.

Sammy turned and put his other hand in Cecilia's. "Let's go, CeCe," he said. "This day is going to be so much fun!"

CHAPTER 21

CECILIA

The rest of the day passed in an awkward truce. Cecilia and Marcus were together but not together. They never spoke. Sammy was oblivious. He would hold both their hands, so it almost looked like Cecilia and Marcus were the little boy's parents.

Toward the end of the day, Sammy went back into the bouncy castle. Cecilia and Marcus stood uncomfortably beside each other, not talking. Finally, Cecilia couldn't stand it any longer.

"Are you ever going to let me explain?" she asked with irritation.

"No explanation necessary," Marcus answered. "A picture tells a thousand words, and all that. You disgust me."

Cecilia was stunned at his words. Tears

came to her eyes. "Then we're even," she said. "Because I disgust myself. Nothing you can say to me or think about me could possibly be worse than what I think about myself. I didn't do what you think I did. I also didn't do what I should have done. But I can tell you this, I have never and would never take advantage of a special needs kid. I tried to help, though I don't expect you to ever believe that."

"You kissed him, didn't you?" Marcus said.

"Yes, I did," Cecilia answered softly.

She wanted to explain the rest of it. How she had tried to get the others to stop. Had tried to protect Remy. But she knew it was futile. Marcus had his mind made up.

"You know, I thought you were a different person," Marcus said. "Guess I was wrong."

"You *are* wrong," Cecilia said. "Just not for the reason you think."

"Whatever," Marcus said. "I'm done thinking and talking about this whole thing. You certainly didn't take long to fit right in with the rest of the step team, did you? They elect you captain after you won the Remy Points game?"

"Actually, I quit the step team. I'm not going

back to Cap Central," Cecilia said. "So this is probably the last time you'll have to see me. I'm not going to go to a school where people are such bullies. Brennay was the worst, but you know what? In your own way, you're a bully too. You've made up your mind about me. You won't listen to my side. I don't know what's wrong with everyone, but you're not nice people. None of you. I'm done with all of you."

She stepped away to wait for Sammy.

Marcus hated hearing her describe him as a bully. He thought of himself as a nicer person than the guy she was describing. It angered him that she was lumping him in with Brennay and others at Cap Central who weren't nice people. He *was* nice, which was why he didn't need to listen to her excuses.

Sammy got out of the bouncy castle, and Marcus could see that the little boy was exhausted. "Come on, buddy, we've done it all," he said. "Let's go home."

"Can CeCe come with us?" Sammy asked.

"No, I have to go to my own house," Cecilia answered. "But I'll see you next week, okay?" She knelt down and gave Sammy a hug.

"I love you, CeCe," the little boy said tiredly.

"I love you too, Sammy," she answered. "I'll see you later, okay?"

"Okay," Sammy said.

Marcus pulled the little boy away and turned to leave without saying anything more.

Cecilia watched them go. She knew it would be the last time she would talk to Marcus. He was the first person from Cap Central she had met when she had moved to Lyman Place. She knew things were over between them, and it made her sad.

After the last family had left, Cecilia stayed to help clean up. Mrs. Reynolds took her aside.

"How did things work out with Sammy and his cousin?" she asked.

"Kind of awkward, but it was okay," Cecilia answered.

"Did you run into his cousin at Cap Central?" the older woman asked.

"Sort of," Cecilia said. "Ironically, we had sort of gone out before this whole thing happened. But he's turned against me almost more than anyone else. So today was doubly awful."

"I'm so sorry," Mrs. Reynolds said sympathetically. "Well, if you don't go back to Cap Central, you won't have to run into him again."

"Except that he lives half a block from me!" Cecilia sighed.

"Well, that could be a problem," Mrs. Reynolds said. "Anyway, thanks for all your help today. I meant what I said when I was speaking to Sammy's cousin. You're a valuable member of our Crossroads family. I hope when you're applying to colleges, you'll ask me to write you a recommendation. I have no reservations about doing so. You'll make a fine special education teacher one day."

Cecilia hugged her. "Thanks," she said. "That means so much to me."

She finished cleaning up and headed for home. Cecilia walked into her house and sank onto the couch.

"Tired?" her mother said knowingly.

"Exhausted," Cecilia corrected her.

"Pizza for dinner sound good?" her mother asked, holding the phone.

Cecilia agreed. Her mother phoned in the order, and then asked her daughter about the day.

Cecilia had just started talking when their doorbell rang.

"Wow!" her mother said. "That was quick."

"I'll go," Cecilia said. She took the money her mother handed her and went to answer the door.

Standing on the front lawn was the Cap Central step team. They were dressed in their light blue T-shirts and white shorts, except for Marcella Ortiz, who was wearing a red T-shirt and purple shorts.

As Cecilia watched, they did one of their routines. They stepped with their usual precision. All except for Marcella. Whatever way she was supposed to turn, she would turn the opposite. She would walk into the girls on either side of her. She even caused Valeria to fall dramatically to the ground.

Cecilia couldn't help but laugh. When they were done, Marcella stepped forward. "We need you back," she said. "Obviously! Unless you want us to step like this all year. This is your spot, and you need to be in it. Will you come back?"

The other girls all started yelling. "Please!" and "We need you!" and "Come back to us!"

Cecilia looked at the rows of girls. She could

feel her mother standing behind her. "Seems like a few girls are missing," Cecilia said.

"Yep, our former captains are gone," Valeria said. "Anyone want to tell Cecilia who our new captains are?"

Kayla Abraham stepped forward. "We'd like you to be co-captain with Marcella and Valeria," she said. "We need to undo the tradition of meanness that the step team has been known for. We think you three are the right people to help us do it."

"But everyone thinks I was part of it," Cecilia said.

"You haven't been in school," Valeria said. "It was Brennay in that picture wearing your CC hair elastic. Zakia took the picture. They've been suspended. And kicked off Stepperz."

"But surely not everyone knows that," Cecilia said, thinking of how Marcus treated her at Crossroads.

"Haters gonna hate," Marcella said. "But we're changing our image. And we need you to help us. Will you come back? Please?"

Cecilia thought for a moment. "I'd love to," she said happily.

The girls cheered.

"Then get in your place," Kayla said. Then she caught herself. She clapped her hand over her mouth. "Sorry! Didn't mean to tell the team captain what to do."

Cecilia laughed. She took her place in line. She started one of the Stepperz chants. "Cap! Central! Stepperz, break it down."

The girls did one of their routines. Without music. And on grass. This time, Marcella did it perfectly. When they were done, Cecilia could hear some of her neighbors clapping.

"Girls, we're getting pizza," Mrs. Calhoun said from the porch. "Will you all stay for a while?"

The girls agreed and came inside the house.

Mrs. Calhoun called to increase the number of pizzas.

When the last girl left, Cecilia flopped on the couch. "I have never been so tired in my life," she said. "Thanks for the pizzas, Mom."

"I was happy to see you with some friends," her mother said. "They seem like really nice girls. And they sure like you a lot."

"I don't actually know when that happened," Cecilia said. "Funny that I had to quit the team for them to start liking me."

"I suspect no one liked what Brennay was doing, but you were the only one brave enough to call her out on it," her mother said. "And once you did, the others felt safe standing up to her too. So you've done some good here. And best of all, you've got some friends."

Cecilia thought about Marcus. "Yeah, it was mostly a good day," she said. She kissed her mother and went to bed.

CHAPTER 22

MARCUS

Marcus heard the step team doing their routine in front of Cecilia's house. He stood on his porch and watched. He saw her come down and join the others.

He checked *Cap Central Chatter* on his computer. The pictures had been taken down. In their place were comments, mostly anonymous. They started out blaming Cecilia and members of the step team for bullying Remy. Then the comments changed.

The pictures were a lie. I was there. You weren't. I know what really happened. I believe in Cecilia. She tried to help Remy. Brennay Baxter is evil.

It was followed by another comment.

It's so sad about Remy. I saw his parents in the main office, waiting to meet with Mrs. Hess. I bet they're gonna take him out of school. And it wasn't his fault. He was the victim in this. Now he's gonna pay the price.

The next comment sounded angrier.

Oh, so now you're all upset about Remy getting bullied. Really? Where were you when this blog was posting those Remy Points? You knew who was behind it. And what did you do to stop it? Nothing. At least that new girl tried to help.

Several other people posted similar messages.

Brennay Baxter hates Cecilia Calhoun because she thinks Thomas Porter likes Cecilia. But Cecilia likes Marcus DiMonte. Brennay faked those pictures to make Cecilia look bad. Don't let a hater win. Cecilia is innocent.

Marcus turned off his computer. He lay

back on his bed and stared at the ceiling. His mind raced with conflicting thoughts. He was so used to feeling anger at Cecilia. It was hard to consider that maybe she was innocent. Yet if those comments were true, Cecilia was a victim too.

Cecilia hadn't been at Cap Central since the pictures came out. It was possible she had been suspended or expelled—for something she might not actually have done. And all because Brennay thought Cecilia had something going on with Thomas Porter.

Marcus knew some of the pictures were real, even if others were fake. He didn't respect Cecilia for having any part of what Brennay did to Remy. But then, he had known Brennay's behavior toward Remy was wrong, and he hadn't done anything either.

He wasn't proud of himself. There were too many times when he should have done the right thing. But he didn't. He knew Brennay was playing with Remy, but he backed off when Remy said he was okay.

He knew Cecilia was a good person, but he immediately doubted her when Brennay posted lies on the blog. He liked Cecilia more than any girl he had ever liked before. Yet he had turned against her without even giving her a chance to explain. His gut had told him the truth about Remy, Brennay, and Cecilia. But instead of listening, he chose to believe the lies.

Marcus had been totally wrong about so much. To make matters worse, he had been horrible to her earlier that day at Crossroads. He'd even tried to get her fired.

He re-read the last comment posted on the blog. This time, he paid more attention to the details. It said that Cecilia liked him. He didn't deserve a second chance. But he knew he had to try.

CHAPTER 23

CECILIA

Cecilia woke up feeling happier than she had since she could remember. It wasn't so much knowing she was the co-captain of the Stepperz. It was that she finally knew she wasn't alone. Other girls had hated what was going on too. They just hadn't spoken up.

As a team captain, she had the ability to turn the step team's reputation around. No more bullying or meanness. And no more publicity photo shoots. It would be hard to change the team's tarnished image. But it had to be done. When she returned to school on Monday, she would talk to the girls about service projects. She wanted them to adopt a cause and work toward it.

There was a tap at her bedroom door. Her

mother opened it. "Oh, good. You're up," she said. "You have a visitor. He's been sitting on the porch swing for a while now."

Cecilia threw off the covers.

"I like him, by the way," her mother said with a smile.

Cecilia brushed her teeth and threw on some jeans. She walked out the front door. Marcus was sitting on the porch swing. An empty plate was on the swing beside him.

"My mother made you breakfast?" she said, rubbing her eyes.

"Yep. Bacon and eggs," he said, putting the plate on the porch floor so there was room on the swing.

"How long have you been out here?" Cecilia asked.

"A while," he admitted. "I wanted to make sure to catch you before you went anywhere. Can you sit?"

Cecilia sat down at the end of the swing. She wondered why he was there.

Marcus didn't say anything. He just rocked the swing back and forth.

Finally, Cecilia stood up. "Well, now that you've had your breakfast, can I go back inside?" she asked.

"Sit, please?" Marcus asked. "I'm trying to figure out how to start."

Cecilia sat back down.

"I just wanted to tell you that I was an idiot. I believed the worst about you, even though I should have known better. I'm trying to say I'm sorry. I hope we can be friends again some time."

"So yesterday you were trying to get me fired, and today you want to be friends?" Cecilia asked, annoyed. "What changed your mind? Oh, wait, I know. You saw that the Stepperz forgave me. So once again, instead of making up your own mind, you accepted someone else's opinion. In this case, the fifteen or so girls on the step team."

Marcus shook his head. "I know that's what it looks like," he said. "I can't defend what I did. I believed those pictures, even though I knew you well enough to know you wouldn't have done any of those things to Remy. I hate myself for it. And you're right about me accepting someone else's opinion. You were just wrong about whose opinion swayed me."

Cecilia was almost too angry to respond. "So who did you listen to this time?" she asked.

"Sammy," Marcus said, smiling. "He adores you. And he's a pretty good judge of character. Better, apparently, than I am."

"Sammy likes everybody," Cecilia said, sitting back against the swing.

"That's true," Marcus agreed. "But he *really* likes you."

Cecilia didn't say anything. The creak of the swing was the only sound.

"And I do too," Marcus said.

Cecilia looked at him. She felt her eyes fill with tears. The past several weeks had been so terrible, and now everything was turning around.

"I'm so sorry," Marcus said softly.

Cecilia buried her face in her hands. After a few moments, she looked up. "I have a question, and you have to promise me you'll tell me the truth," she said seriously.

"I promise," Marcus said. "Ask me anything."

"How come she made you bacon?" she asked. "I never get bacon!"

"Want some? I seem to have some pull with your mom," Marcus said, grinning.

"In a minute," Cecilia said. She leaned over and rested her head on his shoulder.

Marcus put his arm around her and pulled her close.

The swing rocked back and forth.

WANT TO KEEP READING?

Turn the page for a sneak peek at Leslie McGill's next book in the Cap Central series: *Hero*.

ISBN: 978-1-68021-046-0

NINA

Charlie Ray threw his pencil down on the desk. "Seriously?" he complained.

Lights flashed in the hallway. A mechanized voice said, "There is an emergency in the building. Please proceed to the nearest exit."

"Mrs. Maher, can we just stay here?" Nina Ambrose asked. "You know it's another false alarm."

"Unfortunately, we can't," Mrs. Maher said. "If we're outside too long to finish the exam, I'll give you more time. Let's line up."

Nina put down her pencil and got in line with the rest of the class. She was in the middle of writing a long answer to an essay question on *The Grapes of Wrath*. She didn't want to lose her train of thought.

She picked up her purse and automatically checked to make sure she had a small notebook and a pen. As a reporter for the *Star*, Capital Central High School's online newspaper, she was always on the lookout for a good story.

"This stuff is starting to really scare me," Keisha Jackson said, walking beside Nina. "All these false alarms? And so many thefts lately. My phone last week. Marcus DiMonte's wallet. I've heard other kids have had stuff stolen too. It just seems like—oh my gosh! Is that smoke?"

The hallway was filling with smoke. Students started running. Some started pushing to get down the stairs.

Jair Nobles stood at the top of the stairwell. "Hey, chill!" he said to one boy who was racing to get around the crush of students. "You've got time. Take it easy. Don't want anybody to get hurt, man!"

"Hey, J!" Keisha said, stopping at the top of the stairs. Students tried to push past her. "This looks bad. You coming?"

"Yeah, I'm out of here," Jair said, walking down the stairs with her. "Can't believe all this smoke. I about fell over when I went to the bathroom and found it on fire."

"You discovered the fire?" Nina asked. "What happened?"

"Hey, Nina, move it!" Chance Ruffin said rudely, pushing past her.

"Can I talk to you later?" Nina asked Jair as she moved down the stairs.

"I'll see you outside," Jair yelled over the heads of the other students.

Nina and Keisha walked outside and found their class.

"There you are," Mrs. Maher said. "Okay, everyone's present. No talking. And stay with the class, please."

The teacher walked over to Mrs. Dominguez, the principal's secretary, to turn in her attendance list. As soon as she did, Nina and Keisha left the group. They joined Joss White, Eva Morales, and Neecy Bethune.

A light drizzle was falling. "Of course the day there's an actual fire, it rains," Eva Morales said, pulling her hoodie up over her head. "We're going to be out here forever."

In the distance, they could hear sirens.

"Hey, this is crazy, right?" Jair said, joining the group of girls.

"So tell me," Nina said, pulling out her notebook. "Give me the details. What did you see? Do you know who set it? Everything."

"This gonna be on the test?" Jair joked.

"I'm writing an article on all the stuff that's been happening," Nina said. She hadn't even thought about writing an article until the fire alarm rang. "Stolen phones and wallets, false fire alarms, and now a real fire. I don't know if it's all related. Or just lots of people doing a lot of bad stuff."

"You gonna describe me as the handsome hero of the story?" Jair asked with a smile.

"You'll always be my hero," Keisha said, kissing him on the forehead.

Keisha was president of the student government association. She had been at a party a few months back that had quickly turned rowdy. Word had spread on social media. Soon the house had been overrun with partiers. She had been surrounded by some guys who were trying to force her to drink. Jair and Zander Peterson, who was now her boyfriend, helped her escape.

Nina rolled her eyes. "Please," she said, dragging out the word. "So what happened?" she asked impatiently.

"No big deal," Jair said modestly. "I had to go, you know? So I went to the second floor boys' restroom. Some guys walked out as I went in. The trash bin was on fire. I told Doctor Miller. She hit the alarm. And here we are."

"Who were the guys walking out?" Nina asked him curiously.

"I didn't really pay attention, except for—"

Just then, the doors to the school opened. Two figures dressed in black walked out.

"I was just about to say, except for Kaleb Black. And there he is!"

"Really?" Joss said, looking concerned. "You need to tell someone."

They all looked across the parking lot. Kaleb Black and Bellamy Knight stood apart from the rest of the students. They both held notebooks. They were staring intently at the other kids.

"I wonder where the 'Black Knights' were hiding up till now?" Keisha asked, making quote marks with her fingers. "Shouldn't they have been out here with everyone else?"

Nina checked the time on her cell phone and wrote a note in her notebook. "Weird that they took so long to get out of the school," she agreed.

"You want to know who's doing stuff around here?" Jair said, watching the two dark figures. "I'd keep my eye on them."

Eva shivered. "They scare me," she said. "Ever since they started calling themselves the Black Knights, they've gotten stranger and stranger. Have you noticed how they are always watching everyone and writing in their little notebooks? It's like they're taking notes on all of us. I see them in the cafeteria, watching and writing away. What do you think they're up to?"

"I'd love to see one of their notebooks some-day," Nina said. "Who knows what they've got written in there."

"Or what they're planning," Jair said darkly.

"They just look so ... threatening," Joss said, struggling to find the words. "I mean, wear-ing black is one thing. But ever since Bellamy hacked off her hair, she's just a hot mess."

"And that cape Kaleb wears? And those boots? The chains actually clank when he walks," Keisha added.

"You guys looking at the BKs?" Zander Peterson asked, walking up to the group. He put his arm around Keisha and kissed her.

As if he had heard Zander, Kaleb Black looked their way. He was scowling. He said something to Bellamy Knight and pointed.

Bellamy ran her fingers through what was left of her jet-black hair. It stood straight up on her head in some places. Other sections were cut so close she was almost bald. She looked directly at Jair. She nodded at something Kaleb said and wrote in her notebook.

"Well, that was freaky," Jair said nervously. "Am I on their list or something?"

"It's like they knew we were talking about them," Joss said with a shiver.

"If I had to pick two people who had something to do with this fire ..." Keisha said.

"Something's going on around here lately," Jair said. "Something not good."

Nina made a few more notes in her notebook.

"I agree," she said. "And I'd sure like to figure out who's behind it."

They all turned again to look at Kaleb and Bellamy.

"You're looking at them," Jair said.

ABOUT THE AUTHOR

Leslie McGill was raised in Pittsburgh. She attended Westminster College (Pa.) and American University in Washington, D.C. She lives in Silver Spring, Maryland, a suburb of Washington, D.C., where she works in a middle school. She lives with her husband, a newspaper editor, and has two adult children.

2 1982 02880 3082